MURDER ROCKS THE BOAT

MURDER ROCKS THE BOAT

LINDA SHIRLEY ROBERTSON

Coastal Villages Press
Beaufort, South Carolina

Tabby Manse

Published by Coastal Villages Press,
a division of Tabby Manse, Inc.,
PO Box 6300, Beaufort, SC 29903,
843-524-0075, fax 843-525-0000,
a publisher of books since 1992.
Visit our web site: www.coastal-villages.com.

Available at special discounts for bulk purchases
and sales promotions from the publisher
and your local bookseller.

Cover photograph and design by Barbara Martin

ISBN 1-882943-24-4

First Edition
Printed in the United States of America

This one is for Meredith,
the Southern belle
whose steel magnolia spirit
grew to be as strong
as the moss-laden live oaks
of our lowcountry

Acknowledgments

I would like to give a special thanks to my editor and friend, Barbara Martin, and my Beaufort writing group, especially Sharon McGee. I also need to mention how much I appreciate the support of my Greenville family and friends.

Part of this book was written on a retreat in St. Petersburg, Florida. Thanks to Rick, Sarah, Duncan, and Luna.

The Beaufort library gave me access to information when I needed to do research, and they always helped me with a willing spirit and a friendly smile.

Without a cool retreat to Canada with Blanche, Guy, Clark, and my friend Sharon, I would still be writing. Thanks for the wonderful support and artful suggestions.

To Hank, Amy, Addie, and Cocoa, I thank you for sharing your knowledge on the Civil War.

Linda Shirley Robertson

Murder Rocks the Boat

"Don't be afraid to rock the boat. It's better than sinking in it."

Suze Orman
O, The Oprah Magazine
August 2004

One

Hannah Jane Graham rested her elbow on the banister rail and stared out at the salt marshes. She watched a brown pelican circle and then dive with a clumsy plop into the water. When it surfaced, she could see a fish wriggling in its pointed beak. Except for the pelicans' splashes or an occasional squawk from a heron waiting at the water's edge for dinner to swim by, everything was quiet. The scene reminded her of a nature documentary she had seen not long ago.

Maggie Stewart walked down the stairs of her newly renovated cottage so quietly that Hannah didn't notice her until she spoke. "When I decided I wanted to live on Seaward Island, this cottage wasn't my first choice," Maggie said, pushing an unruly lock of sun-streaked hair out of her eyes. "I was upset when I found out I couldn't buy the house on the beach next to Marilyn and Greg Meyers. But now I'm glad it happened that way. Their house is on the market, and they've moved to Aspen. Greg has a new practice out there."

The two women stared in silence at the view for a few minutes more and then walked back to the top of the stairs and stood on the veranda. Even though it was October, the weather was pleasantly warm, and the sun glinted off a wall of windows, causing Maggie to squint.

"The cream window frames are perfect with your bead-board paneling and the deep reds in your area rug," Hannah commented. "Are the pine floors original?"

Maggie shrugged. "We think so. This was a caretaker's residence for the Heyward Plantation. John Heyward's family has owned this land for generations. It was easy for me to buy it from them, since

John and I are…were…" Maggie hesitated, searching for the right word. "Close," she said finally.

Hannah faced Maggie with a frown. "I still don't understand why you wanted to have your own place. Aren't you and John still together?"

Maggie couldn't help but feel a little sad. "We're seeing other people for a while," she said. Then she brushed the subject away impatiently and waved toward the marshes. "This is yours while you're here."

Maggie led Hannah through double French doors into a guest bedroom. "My carpenter, Cotton Wellford, built the veranda. He's the best. He'll be back Monday to finish the sleeping porch. The wicker chairs and side table are temporary until I decide how to furnish it. You can have your morning coffee and watch the egrets and osprey dive for breakfast in Lawson Creek. This side of Seaward is remote. Even the people in the gated community on the other side of the island don't know we're here. This is my slice of paradise."

Hannah took her friend's hands with a smile. "I was ecstatic when you called Rosemont Interiors," she said. "Your plan and presentation boards for this Ribaut Inn project in Beaufort are fantastic. Thanks for asking me to come."

Hannah gave Maggie a quick hug and then turned her attention to unpacking a duffle bag on a suitcase holder by the window. "The flowers on the table smell very Southern somehow, but I can't quite place the scent," she commented as she pulled out a hairdryer.

Maggie laughed. "It's Mama's crazy gardenia bush I brought from Rosemont. It blooms almost year-round down here. I like to keep fresh flowers in the house. The flowers in the kitchen are Oriental lilies that Robert buys for his restaurant."

Possum, Maggie's yellow Lab, came bounding into the room. She had fallen asleep chewing on a bone about an hour ago, and now she was ready for some attention. Maggie bent to scratch the dog behind the ears, which caused Possum's backside to wiggle with delight.

Hannah smiled at the dog's antics and turned to finish unpacking. She caught sight of her reflection in a mahogany mirror above a bow-front chest. *I look a little rumpled*, she thought, smoothing her short skirt. She studied her face in the mirror briefly. She still looked youthful, especially when she smiled, she decided, and she was tall—taller than Maggie. But no matter how hard she exercised, she remained a bit bottom heavy.

Possum didn't like being ignored, so she licked Hannah's hand. "Take the dog out, and I'll finish unpacking," she said. Maggie turned to leave, but Hannah stopped her with a question. "By the way, are there any good looking men on Seaward? I'm not interested in any of the good ol' boys, mind you. We have those in Rosemont."

Maggie mentally filed through the names of all the men she knew on the island. Most of them were rejected quickly. But then she remembered someone who might interest Hannah. "Robert Davis is old enough to be our father," she said, "but he's settled in a beach-front house that I redid for him. He's lots of fun, and he just opened the Palmetto Bluff Marina and the Tabby Café next door to it. The chef is from Georgetown, but I just met him briefly. Only other possibility is Bill Johnson, the substitute sheriff we have while Sheriff Hammond is on vacation. Don't suppose we'll see him, though," Maggie added thoughtfully. "Seaward is a quiet little island."

Hannah sighed dramatically to show her disappointment. "At least I have choices," she said ruefully. "Now take Possum out, and I'll be down as soon as I unpack. We'll go over the Ribaut Inn presentation."

"Come on, Poss. Let's go." The Lab followed her out of the room and down the stairs.

In less than half an hour, Hannah found Maggie and Possum in the kitchen. Maggie was sitting at the table, thumbing through a magazine, and Possum sat quietly with her head in Maggie's lap.

"I just talked to Robert," Maggie announced. "He's loaning me his marina boat to finish my lessons with Salty George. I'm learning to pilot a boat so I don't have to depend on the Mary Grace for transportation to the mainland. That ferry is always late, and Randy and Dianne don't have any excuse." She rolled her eyes. "They must sleep late every day."

Hannah's eyes opened wide. "You're going to haul me around these islands on a boat?" she protested. "Do you really think you know what you're doing?"

Maggie answered with a laugh. "My plan is to sell the Volvo, buy a golf cart, and try to find a used boat that will be practical in our waters but not too big to handle. If we get the Ribaut Inn job, I'll be able to afford a boat and an old used car to leave at the Beaufort marina."

Hannah rummaged in the refrigerator until she found a can of diet cola. "You decided not to get the glass door style I told you about," she commented, indicating the refrigerator with a nod.

Maggie shook her head. "Can you imagine how clean I'd have to keep the shelves if I had glass doors on it? And when anyone came in, they could see everything in there. And I couldn't just leave plain ol' catsup bottles for the world to see. I'd have to buy containers to match the kitchen." She threw up her hands in mock exasperation. "A granite-based pump bottle for the Dijon? I don't think so."

"It is a trend," Hannah insisted, "and we have to keep up with those. Mary Jo in Rosemont wanted one. Don't know how she heard about glass door refrigerators. Or about the business of putting a urinal in her renovated bathroom. Mike said he wanted one, and I've got it ordered."

"Well, I'm glad one of us is keeping up with the latest trends," Maggie said with a chuckle. "And I'm glad you're here for a couple of weeks. But you can forget about orders and complaints from Rosemont interiors for now." She glanced out the window and smiled. "I'm certainly glad I decided to sell out and move to this part of the world."

Hannah flipped the tab on her cola with her index finger, then examined her nail closely to make sure she hadn't marred her manicure. "It is beautiful here," she admitted, but she wondered silently how Maggie could stand to leave the city and move to such a dull place. Once you got your fill of sunshine and wildlife, what was there to do for fun? There were few gourmet restaurants and food shops, unless you were willing to drive to Charleston or Savannah, no Macy's or Bloomingdale's, and, worst of all, few good-looking, eligible men, apparently. Hannah decided it was best to change the subject. "What's our schedule?" she asked.

"We have our first meeting this evening with Chandler Morris at the Inn," Maggie answered. "We'll give him our presentation and find out if he's interested. I'm excited about our first job. If this clicks, you may want to consider coming into Lowcountry Interiors as my partner." Maggie looked up at her friend hopefully. "Is that a good name for it?"

Hannah cleared her throat, giving herself time to think how she would dodge the question. "There are probably a million design firms named that in this area, but it'll do for now," she said.

"We'll need to catch the Mary Grace at five o'clock. That should give us plenty of time to make the appointment."

"Maybe I should start getting ready," Hannah said, glancing at her watch. "I don't think I'll need a suit for an evening presentation. What are you wearing?"

Maggie shrugged. "Haven't thought about it. Probably a pair of black jeans, white cotton pullover sweater and my boat shoes. I'll bring my nicer shoes in a briefcase, which happens to be a big Kate Spade bag. I dumped my leather briefcase when I moved here."

Hannah let out a wail, startling Possum, who lifted her head from Maggie's lap, stared at Hannah a moment, and wailed, too. "I don't have anything like that," Hannah shouted over Possum's howls. "Why didn't you tell me how informal you are around here? We'll have to go shopping. Do we have time to do a run to Saks in Charleston?"

Maggie shook her head. "You can borrow a black skirt from me. I have a better project for us. It'll make me and Possum feel better."

Hannah looked at her friend doubtfully. "Project? I don't like the sound of that. I don't have to build anything, do I?" She looked down at her French manicure and frowned.

"It's here in the kitchen," Maggie said. "Over there at the door. Cotton installed a doggie door for Possum. I can leave her while we're away, and she can run out to the fenced area in the back yard and then back into the house. There's only one problem with it: Possum won't use it. We are going to teach her how to come in and go out of the doggie door. When Cotton comes back Monday, he'll be delighted to see she's learned how to use it."

Hannah sighed. "Okay," she said. "I'll stand here while you point to the door. Come on, Possum. Go through the door."

Maggie chuckled. "That's not going to work. I've tried that. You are going outside and crawl through the door. I'll be inside calling Possum, and she'll follow you through the door."

Hannah looked at Maggie as if she'd lost her mind. "You're kidding, right? Crawl through that little hole?" Hannah examined Maggie's face, watching hopefully for a smile. When she saw Maggie was serious, she added, "Really now, why don't you crawl through while I stand here and call her? That sounds to me like the best way to handle this."

"Afraid not," Maggie answered. "She won't come if you call her. She'll come if I'm inside holding a meaty bone. We shouldn't have to do it more than four or five times. She's a smart puppy."

Hannah glanced around the kitchen as though she were looking for an escape route. "I came down here to give you a boost and help with a presentation for a new client. I didn't sign up for crawling through a doggie door on all fours."

Maggie stood up and shooed Hannah and Possum toward the door. She held it open and looked sternly at them both. "Out, out," she commanded. "I'll get her bone. Start crawling." Maggie shut the door and started for a canister she kept on her granite countertop. She stopped in mid-stride when the telephone rang, grabbing it on the second ring and ignoring shouts from just outside the back door.

She recognized Robert's voice and chatted with him briefly before she was interrupted by a new commotion. She turned, resting the phone against her shoulder, and realized that Hannah had tried to crawl through the doggie door, as instructed, but hadn't quite made it. Her upper body was in the kitchen, but her hips seemed to be wedged tightly. Hannah struggled mightily to push her way inside, and when that didn't work, to back out of the doggie door, but she was stuck. The flap over the doggie door puffed into the air with every movement and landed with a thwap on Hannah's face. "Help me!" she shouted. "Possum is licking my feet! Ugh!"

Maggie brought the phone back to her ear. "Hey, Robert," she said, trying to keep a straight face, "I have to get Hannah out of the doggie door. She's making quite a fuss, and I can't really hear you. I'll talk to you in a while."

Maggie put down the phone. She glanced out the window and saw that Possum had lost interest in the entire project. The Lab had found a favorite toy and was chewing it contentedly, sprawled comfortably on the grass.

"Say," Maggie said cheerily, "that toy wasn't there last night, and I didn't take it out. Possum must have taken it out herself. She has learned to use the doggie door after all!"

From the stream of curses coming from just inside the doggie door, Maggie could tell that Hannah was unimpressed.

"Stay where you are!" Maggie commanded. "I'll get you out of there."

"Does it look like I have a choice?" Hannah snarled.

Maggie sat on the floor, grabbed Hannah's hands, and braced her feet against the door. With a grunt, she heaved Hannah with all her strength. On the third pull, Hannah popped through. She picked herself up with as much dignity as she could muster, glaring at Maggie and daring her to laugh. "That dog can just stay outside," she grumped.

At that instant, Possum came barreling through the doggie door, nearly bowling Hannah over. Hannah frowned down at the dog for a minute; then she started to laugh. "She watched me do it and she got it on the first try," Hannah said proudly. "She deserves her bone now."

Hannah hobbled over to a chair and plopped down while Maggie dug out a bone for Possum.

"That was Robert Davis on the phone," Maggie said. "He needs for me to return the Seaward Lady. It'll be great practice for a quick boat ride. I'm supposed to take her out again before my next lesson. Want to come?"

"Tell me more about Robert." Hannah tried to sound casual, but Maggie noted that she reached for her purse on the kitchen table, pulled out a compact and lipstick, and coated her full lips with shiny pink gloss. "Do I look okay to meet him, do you think?" Maggie opened her mouth to answer, but Hannah kept talking. "I do want to meet all the people you've mentioned in your e-mails. I like to put names with faces."

Hannah ran a comb through her hair and followed Maggie out the door. Maggie decided not to mention that the wind whipping around the sides of the boat would destroy any hairdo. Hannah would learn soon enough that natural was the only way to go on Seaward.

Maggie and Hannah walked through the yard and onto the dock. It was short compared with most of the docks in the area. Maggie's cottage sat on high ground near deep water. The Heywards of this generation thought maybe the place had been a storage area before it was used to house a caretaker, and it was probably once a loading dock for rice that was grown on the plantation and shipped out by boat.

"This has got to be the best view on the East Coast," Hannah said. "October in the upstate of South Carolina means things start cooling off and the leaves are turning. Do you like living in a place that doesn't have changing seasons?"

"We have seasonal changes here. See?" Maggie pointed to marsh grass along the water's edge. "The bottom of the grass is green, but the top is already brown. In a few weeks, it'll all be a vibrant gold, and the centipede grass in the yard will turn, too. Dormant in the winter. Sea Islands are golden in the winter and a lush green in the summer. Living on a tidal creek gives me a beautiful view all year. Look, there's a snowy egret waiting for dinner."

The women reached the end of the dock, and Maggie untied the cleats and hopped aboard. Hannah jumped in after her.

"Do you know what you're doing?" Hannah asked nervously. "How many boat lessons have you had?"

Maggie ignored the question. She flipped the blower switch and waited a second before the Yamaha outboard roared to life. "Sit next to me under the canopy and put this cap on," she told Hannah. "You'll get too much sun, even on this short ride. It's about ten minutes to Palmetto Bluff from here. Shorter walk from the house, but we have to go around this huge sandbar. It's tricky on the coast. I'm learning to read the maps as well as the GPS."

Hannah shook her head in bewilderment. "Sounds like an airport," she said. "What's a GPS?"

"It's a way to always tell where you are."

Maggie tried to explain the technical aspects of the system, but Hannah waved away the explanation.

"Never mind. I'll leave this up to you and enjoy the ride."

Maggie gazed out across the sparkling water and saw dark fins surface a few yards away. "Look, the dolphins are swimming out here today."

Hannah watched, wide-eyed, as one of the dolphins leaped into the air. She clapped her hands with delight. "I'm beginning to see why you like this place," she said.

Maggie smiled at her friend. She remembered having the same reaction the first time she saw dolphins swimming in the wild. She had been as excited as a child. "Sometimes you can actually spot them along the river walk downtown," she commented.

"Do you ever see sharks?" Hannah asked with a shiver.

"I've seen little sand sharks near the shore, but I've never heard of anyone being bitten. The big boys usually stay out in open water." Maggie slowed the boat down. "See that house on the hill?"

Hannah squinted against the bright sunshine. "It looks like a fort," she said. "Must be old."

"Not really. In the early fifties, a group that liked to hunt deer decided to purchase the property and build something similar to an Irish hunting lodge. Their heirs rent it out to certain families. Since the Heywards got the law changed, no one is allowed to hunt on Seaward. I heard Paul Morgan—you've heard of him, right? The best-selling author?"

Hannah shook her head.

"The guy that wrote *Murder in the Afternoon*? They made it into a movie starring Ethan Hawke."

"Oh, yeah, now I remember. Ethan Hawke is gorgeous!"

"Well, anyway," Maggie continued, "I heard that Paul Morgan is renting it for the winter. He's supposed to be writing another book. Robert says he eats at the café all the time."

Hannah grabbed her purse and dug through its contents for her compact. "I saw Paul Morgan on *60 Minutes* once. He was a knockout! Does he have a wife?" Maggie shrugged. "Well, do I look okay?"

Maggie gave her friend an indulgent grin. "What's the matter with you? I thought you had all the dates you could handle in Rosemont."

"That's the way I intend to keep it," Hannah retorted. "It's been five years since my divorce, and I'm not ready to settle down yet." She wrinkled her nose, looking like she had caught a whiff of a horseshoe crab rotting in the sun. "'Course, if you'd been married to a man whose mama wouldn't let you keep any of the family silver, you'd understand."

Maggie shook her head. It was hard to tell when Hannah was kidding and when she was serious. She powered the boat toward the pier at the Tabby Café and saw Chef Jim stick his head out the back door of the café. He looked toward the boat and waved. Hannah would melt in a puddle when she met him, Maggie was sure. Maggie gave Jim a quick wave and concentrated on docking the Seaward Lady. She had practiced this maneuver at least a dozen times last week with Salty George. *Piece of cake*, she thought. She cut back on the throttle and began to nose the boat into a marina slip. The current sent waves splashing against the hull of the boat, making a thumping sound. Then she felt a bump on the side of the boat she had never experienced before.

"Sit still," she said to Hannah. "Something isn't right with this slip. I'm going to try to put it in reverse and move to the one next to us."

Hannah was instantly in a panic. "Something's wrong? We're not sinking, are we? Tell me I'm going to have a chance to meet some of these men you've told me about before I die!"

Maggie put the boat into reverse, but it wouldn't move. A sailboat came about in Lawson Creek and sent waves through the heavy current, causing the Seaward Lady to rock. "I've got to go up on the bow..." Seeing Hannah's blank expression, she amended, "...to the front to see what's keeping this boat from going into the slip. I can't get it to go either way. A log or a piece of driftwood must be in the way."

Hannah followed Maggie to the bow, swaying and reeling with the movement of the boat. She looked over the side, blinked, and looked again. An expression of horror came over her face. She took a deep breath and fainted. She tumbled over the side and into the chilly water.

Robert had seen Maggie's dilemma and ran toward the boat. He grabbed the rope and secured the Boston Whaler. Then he turned his attention to Hannah, but she had already surfaced, gagging and sputtering. Her hair was plastered over her eyes, and her clothes were full of sand and soaked with salty water.

Maggie couldn't help but laugh. "What's the matter?" she asked. "My parking job too scary for you?"

She reached down to help her friend onto the dock, but instead she screamed and fell into the water next to Hannah—right on top of the corpse of her carpenter, Cotton Wellford.

Two

aggie's head popped to the surface. She took a deep breath and made it to the dock in two strokes. Hannah was already putting her hand up, reaching for Bill Johnson's outstretched arms.

Sheriff Hammond was at a fishing tournament in the Gulf, and he had told everyone that he was going to visit family in Old Indian Pass, Florida, before he returned. Because Bill was a former sheriff from Raleigh, the chief had hired him to keep an eye on Seaward, with instructions to just make sure the deputies kept moving through the county. Everyone knew that Bill spent most of his time fishing or shooting the breeze at the Tabby Café, and for once, his presence at the café was a godsend.

Hannah took just a little longer than necessary to let go of Bill's arms. Even a floating corpse couldn't keep her from noticing Bill's brown, curly hair and his impressive biceps.

Maggie, on the other hand, only wanted to get out of the water. She crawled onto the dock and tried to stand up. She swayed and stumbled and felt a pair of strong arms wrap around her. She looked up into Robert Davis' face. She looked around, still dazed, to find a group of snowbirds staring at her, wide-eyed. These Northerners, who wintered here every year, would certainly have something to tell their neighbors when they went home in the spring, Maggie thought. They pressed closer, eager to see what was happening, but Bill waved them back.

"Everybody stand back," he shouted. He turned to Robert. "I'll call it in and get some officers out here to protect the scene. You take these ladies into your office and see if you can find them some dry clothes. I'll talk to them in a little while."

25

Robert nodded and put his arms protectively around the two women's shoulders as he led them away. Jim met them at the door and held it open. He helped Maggie to a seat. Jim had always treated Maggie with special consideration when she came to the café. He always made sure she had an extra delicacy on her plate not available to other patrons. As he knelt in front of her, Maggie could see he was worried. "Are you okay?" he asked, and his voice shook.

Maggie gave him a weak nod. "We just need to get dry, and I'd like to make some phone calls," she said.

Jim took Maggie by the arm and helped her up. "Come on," he said. "I'll take you to Robert's office in back."

Maggie glanced over her shoulder to check on Hannah, who was trailing behind. In different circumstances, she might have laughed at her friend's bedraggled appearance. Hannah had lost a shoe, and she looked cold and miserable. There was no trace of the sexy pink lip gloss, and the remains of her mascara ran down her cheeks and dripped off her chin.

"What happened?" Jim asked as they walked toward the back of the café. "Did you wreck the boat on the dock? Is that what all the excitement is about?"

"It's much worse than that," Maggie answered. She began to explain, but the more she talked, the more upset she became. Cotton Wellford had been, not just her favorite carpenter, but a friend. She was shaking uncontrollably as she walked into Robert's office, and when she looked around, everything reminded her of Cotton. Robert had hired Maggie to decorate his office, and Cotton had built the bookcases that lined the walls. Maggie remembered that Cotton had loved the mahogany library table and the antique Turkish carpet she had chosen. He said they made the office feel like a private retreat.

Maggie ran her hands slowly over the bookcases and said to no one in particular, "He did a good job on these."

26

Jim handed the two women towels. "Is there anything else I can do?" he asked. When both women assured him they were fine, he turned to go. But then he turned back and gave Maggie a sympathetic look. "I'm sorry I didn't get to know Cotton better. Always thought I'd ask him to go fishing or something." He walked out with his head bowed.

Maggie and Hannah scrounged some shirts from Robert's closet and got out of their wet clothes. Robert knocked on the door to make sure they were decent before he walked in. "I see you like my Hawaiian shirts," he said with a grin. "Look like dresses on you, though."

Maggie barely heard him.

"What's going on?" she demanded. "Do they know what happened? Did Cotton fall in, hit his head, and drown?"

Robert ignored the question. "Come on," he said. "I'm driving you home." He herded the women out the door and through the parking lot toward his Chrysler convertible. Gossips on the island whispered that it had cost a fortune to bring it over on a barge. The top was down, and Maggie slipped into the seat beside him. He turned the ignition key, and it was only then that Maggie noticed Hannah was missing. She looked around frantically for her friend.

Robert chuckled. "She's gone to have another gander at Hammond's stand-in," he said.

Maggie stepped out of the car and called to Hannah. When Hannah finally limped, sans one shoe, to the car and climbed in, she didn't sound nearly as traumatized as she looked. "He says we'll get together soon. He's just waiting for the coroner to get here. I told him to come by your house and have a drink if he wanted more information from us." She paused to catch her breath before adding, "Isn't he the most gorgeous hunk of a man? And only two years older than me and from North Carolina."

Robert shook his head in amazement. "How do women get so much info in such a short time?" he asked. His expression became grim when he turned to face his passengers. "Cotton was stabbed with a fishing knife." He hesitated briefly before adding, "Lots of times."

Maggie groaned and covered her eyes.

Robert took a deep breath and continued. "Then he was thrown into the water, tied to the dock, and left for the fishes. Who in the world would want to kill Cotton? He just did his job—and a darn good one—and kept to himself."

A bright red SUV Explorer whizzed past and skidded into the driveway that led to the dock. Hannah caught a glimpse of a "Sea Time" vanity plate.

"Who's that?" she asked.

Robert snorted. "A day late and a dollar short. There's something wrong with that kid's head. He can't even do a decent license plate."

Hannah turned to Maggie, hoping for an answer that would be more enlightening.

"It's Sherman Pritchard," Maggie told her. "His daddy owned the *Seaward Times*. Sherman is the star reporter, and he's supposed to put the paper to bed every week, but he's usually already asleep. He's not such a bad kid, I guess, but I do wish he would learn to spell."

Hannah nodded. "While I was waiting for the Mary Grace to bring me over, I read last week's paper. He wrote an article about the growth spurt on Seaward. He mentioned your cottage and reported what a great job Cotton had done with the renovations."

Maggie sighed. "He told me he was going to do that. I didn't talk to him, and I didn't know he had talked to Cotton. We need to find out if Cotton said anything to him that might give us a clue to…"

"I don't think so," Robert interrupted gruffly. "You have no business nosing around in this. You should just concentrate on your new business and let the police do their job."

Maggie pursed her lips and patted Robert on the arm. "We'll come over for lunch and talk about this tomorrow." Then her eyes opened wide as she remembered her appointment with a potential client. "Hannah, did you call Chandler Morris at the Ribaut Inn? He was expecting us this evening. I meant to call from Robert's office, but I forgot."

"I changed the appointment to Wednesday afternoon. We'll have a day to recover from all this."

Maggie leaned her head back against the car seat wearily. "It'll take longer than that," she mumbled to herself as Robert steered the car down the driveway to her cottage.

Robert turned down an invitation to come inside. "I'm going back to the café," he said. "Need to do some damage control and get ready for the evening crowd. Are we still on for my wine-tasting party?"

"We'll talk about it at the end of the week," Maggie said without enthusiasm. "Right now, I'm going to take a hot shower and then sit on the porch with a stiff drink in my hand."

Hannah ran inside, and Maggie followed. Possum greeted them enthusiastically as they walked into the kitchen. Maggie tossed the dog a treat and walked upstairs for her shower. Hannah trailed her, still talking about Bill Johnson, but Maggie barely heard the chatter. Maggie stepped into the bathroom and shut the door behind her. Hannah finally went silent, and Maggie savored the peace as she stepped under the hot water and willed herself to relax.

When she had dried off, she pulled on a pair of jeans and a cotton T-shirt. She sat down on her bed and covered her face. How could this have happened to Cotton? She remembered that Cotton had told her he wouldn't be back to work at her house for a day or two.

Did he say he had business in Beaufort? Maggie wished she could remember his exact words.

When she felt she could face Hannah again, she walked downstairs to the kitchen. She found Hannah unpacking a basket of goodies that Jim and Robert had sent from the café. Maggie wasn't hungry, but she poured two glasses of Australian Shiraz and put some meatloaf sandwiches and pecan shortbread from the basket on the Fiesta plates she had inherited from her Aunt Ina.

"Let's eat on the front deck," she said.

Hannah settled in a club chair that Maggie had covered in navy with cream and coral trim.

"The chairs match the sunset tonight," Hannah remarked. She took a bite of the sandwich, made with venison and some unfamiliar but delightful herbs and spices. "That chef from the Tabby is an excellent cook, and he is definitely interested in you. But you don't give him the time of day. How come?"

Maggie took a nibble of her sandwich and put it back on the plate. "I'm thinking about it," she said. "At least he's here. John is always in Montana working on a new conservation plan."

She stared out over Lawson Creek as the coral in the sky turned a bright red. A gentle breeze kept the no-see-ums away, and the view had a calming effect.

Then she turned to Hannah. She had almost forgotten her friend was there. "I'm sorry your first day on Seaward has been upsetting," she said. "We'll get back on track tomorrow. In the morning, we'll sun on the dock, relax, and check our notes for the Ribaut Inn meeting." Maggie took a sip of her wine and mumbled, "Too many people at the marina to figure out what happened."

Hannah looked up in surprise. "You mean to figure out who killed your friend? Bill Johnson is certainly capable of handling that. He told me he'd had three murder cases in Raleigh before he came down here. I think he came for some peace and quiet." Hannah shook her head. "Little did he know."

"You found out a lot about him in a short time," Maggie noted.

"I intend to find out more," Hannah said with a note of determination in her voice. "He also told me he had taught crime courses at Hollins and"—Hannah paused dramatically—"he isn't married!"

Maggie smiled. "I wish I could find out how you do it. Here for less than a day and already on your way to a new relationship."

From inside the house, the phone rang, and Maggie reluctantly rose from her lounger with a grunt. "Be right back," she called over her shoulder.

Hannah grabbed the current issue of *Savannah Magazine* from a stack by her chair. She had intended to read through it to find the best shopping areas. She'd also heard the stores on Hilton Head Island were excellent. She wondered if she could talk Maggie into a shopping trip. Hannah was wandering through an imaginary designer shoe store when Maggie came back and flopped onto the lounger.

"It was Maude, the Heywards' housekeeper," Maggie said. "She heard about Cotton. She's like a mother hen. She took care of me when I got chickenpox a while back. She wanted me to promise to stay out of the murder case." Maggie paused for a gulp of wine. "She thinks he died in some sort of freak accident."

"Accident? Accident?" Hannah exclaimed. "How can it be an accident when the guy has forty-seven million knife wounds in his body?"

"Maude thinks the murderer didn't mean to kill him. She thinks whoever it was just panicked." Maggie waved her arms wearily in the air. "Something like that anyway."

Hannah snorted. "She didn't see the body." She studied Maggie's face for a moment. "What was it you said was keeping John in Montana?"

"He's helping the Friends of the Bison make a sanctuary for buffalo. He's showing them how to make the area into a protective enclave and how to keep hunters away. I think they are paying him for his counsel."

Maggie was silent for a while, her eyes vacant. "I can't figure out a motive," she said abruptly. "I don't think Cotton knew many people in this area. Robert heard a few weeks ago that Cotton was getting a divorce. I didn't even know he was married."

Hannah sighed, knowing there was no getting Maggie's mind off Cotton's death. "Maybe his wife killed him," she said half-heartedly. "Maybe his insurance money would pay more than the divorce settlement."

"I don't think so," Maggie answered. "Robert seemed to think the wife lives in New Mexico." She pushed thoughts of Cotton away abruptly. "Let's not think about it. Bill is being paid to work the case. We need to focus on the Ribaut Inn project."

The women began to discuss the project in earnest, but they were interrupted by ferocious barking from the back yard.

"Is that Possum?" Hannah asked. "Sounds like she's treed a wild animal."

Maggie and Hannah jumped over a stack of boards that Cotton had left in anticipation of finishing the screened-in porch. They raced around the cottage. The full harvest moon beamed a path. Hannah stopped abruptly, and Maggie slammed into her, almost knocking them both over. They stared in bewilderment while Possum raised a commotion at the foot of a gnarled live oak. Maggie looked up through dangling moss, trying to spot what Possum might be excited about, and she saw, with a shiver of panic, a dark figure on a limb just out of Possum's reach.

"Someone hold that dog!" the intruder shouted.

Maggie grabbed Possum by the collar.

"Who the hell is this?" Hannah shrieked.

The two friends watched in wonder as pink satin ballet slippers came into view, following by the strappy nylon netting that held the shoes in place around two shapely ankles.

When the woman finally dropped to the ground, they could see that she was dressed in a cotton batik skirt and an aqua camisole. She had tied netting around her auburn curls, and her pale skin glowed in the moonlight.

The woman faced the startled friends without any apparent embarrassment. "I heard you found Cotton," she said. "I been waitin' forever for you all to come home." When Hannah and Maggie stared at her blankly, she continued her explanation. "I'm Althea. I have the little cottage at the other end of Dolphin Lane. Mr. Heyward's mother let me rent it while I did my sewin'. Made all the slip covers in that plantation house," she added with obvious pride. She waited briefly for a reaction, and when none came, she said, "You must be Maggie. Heard you might need me to do some sewin'."

Maggie finally found her tongue. "This is my friend Hannah Graham, and we need to go sit on the porch and talk about this." She led Althea toward the front of the house. Hannah and Possum followed.

When the three women had settled onto the porch, Althea asked again about Cotton. "It's bad, ain't it? I can tell by your face. His wife, Delores, was here yesterday. Wanted to talk about the divorce and her share of the money." Althea leaned toward Maggie, obviously distressed. "Did she whap him in the head?"

Maggie took a deep breath and reluctantly told Althea what she knew. When she got to the part about finding his body, Althea started to wail. "I knowed it! He had all that money in his pockets. And he wouldn't let me protect him with my white light spell. Said it was just nonsense. Delores killed him and took all his money! You better get that new sheriff man on this right now. Bet Delores is back in New Mexico with poor Cotton's money in her pockets."

The young woman's heavy Southern drawl and her sobs made her story hard to follow, but Maggie thought she got the gist of it. "How much money did he have?" she asked.

Althea looked up in surprise. Tears splashed the freckles sprinkled across her cheeks. "You should know," she said. "He told me it was the money you paid him for finishing this porch." Althea looked around at the stacks of boards and rolls of screen in confusion. When she spotted a stack of tools that had belonged to Cotton, she began to sob again.

Hannah patted Althea's back, trying to calm her down, but Hannah was looking straight at Maggie. "Didn't you tell me..."

Maggie cut her off. "Cotton told me to wait until the job was finished. I never paid him a cent."

Three

O n this Tuesday morning, a balmy breeze feathered waves across the waters of Lawson Creek. Golden brown marsh grass waved in the October sunshine.

Maggie and Hannah sat on the edge of Maggie's dock, dangling their feet in the water. Bill Johnson smiled at Hannah shyly, forgetting for a minute that he was there on official business. Then he cleared his throat and informed Maggie that he had no idea where Cotton could have gotten the money he showed Althea. He opened his mouth to ask Maggie a question, but Hannah smiled at him and he lost his train of thought.

Maggie lost patience and told him everything she knew about the discovery of the body without waiting for his questions. "That's all we know," she concluded. "I suppose it could have been anybody who saw him waving all that money around, but somehow I think it was someone who knew him and not a stranger."

Hannah smiled again, and her pink lip gloss sparkled in the sun. "This area of the world is just full of raw beauty," she cooed. "Oh, look!" She pointed toward the water. "Look, there's a dolphin—no, there's more than one! Looks like they're parading for us."

Bill closed his notebook and slid it and his pen into the back pocket of his worn khaki chinos. "Before I talk to Althea, I need to look at the scene, and I want to talk to Robert. But first I need to have a little lunch. Would you ladies like to join me at the Tabby Café?" The invitation was directed to both women, but his gaze never left Hannah's face.

Maggie started to shake her head, but Hannah spoke up quickly. "Yes," she said breathlessly.

"You two go ahead," Maggie said. "I have some work to do in my office and then I'll try to join you."

Hannah slipped her arm through Bill's as they walked away, headed for the café. Maggie couldn't help but smile. Those two sure did look good together.

Her office faced Lawson Creek, and a wall of windows gave her a view of the sparkling water. She could look up from her computer and watch the fish jump at high tide. This view was much better than the same ol' rolling Atlantic Ocean and a pristine beach, Maggie had decided.

She walked into the office and sat at her wicker desk. The desk had belonged to her maternal grandfather, a doctor. He liked to sit at this desk on his side porch and settle his accounts before he enjoyed a scotch and water. Maggie's mother told her stories about his practice in Rosemont. The chair's back was made of cane; Maggie had found it at the Charleston Flea Market. She had covered the seat with the most expensive material from a designer book and matched the pillows on the linen teal love seat in the opposite corner of this inviting room. She had framed the drapery from her childhood bedroom and hung it on the wall above the sofa. A perfect touch for a designer's office. The room was still evolving, and she had spied a few pieces of art at a gallery in Beaufort that might be perfect in here. If she and Hannah got the Inn job, she could finish the office and look for the right chairs for her dining room.

When she logged on to her computer, she had eight e-mails waiting; three were from John. She answered the messages in the order they were received, trying to keep her mind on business. She didn't want to think about Cotton. He had been the best carpenter she knew, and he had known exactly what this old cottage needed. Did he really have a lot of cash the last time he saw Althea, or was she lying to throw everyone off?

Instead of intruding on Bill and Hannah, Maggie grabbed a protein shake and an apple for lunch and went over her proposal for the Inn. But she couldn't concentrate on work. *Maybe a walk will clear my head,* she thought. She threw Possum a pig's ear to chew on and headed out the door. She wandered without thinking about the direction she would take. When she looked up, she found herself about a mile down a dirt road near Althea's house. John had told her he rented the tiny cottage to Althea in the spring, so Althea hadn't lived on Seaward long enough for most people to get to know her. Had she moved here when Cotton started working on the island?

Maggie rounded a curve in the road and turned in to Althea's driveway. It was too short, really, to be called a road, but a sign announced this was Turtle Lane. The clapboard cottage, covered with vines, sat on a cement foundation. The walkway to the front door was made of sand and oyster shells. The house was quiet. Had Althea run away?

Maggie eased up the creaky steps and across the wooden porch. She peered into the only window that faced the driveway, and she could see through the entire house. The cottage was crammed with tables, chairs, and what Maggie's Grammy had called bric-a-brac. Shards of glass, ceramics, linens, and pots were scattered across nearly every available surface in the front room. Maggie couldn't see a sofa. Maybe Althea had planned to open a flea market on Seaward. Or maybe these were stolen goods. But that wasn't likely, she decided, since most of this stuff wouldn't fetch a dollar in Savannah.

Maggie knocked at the front door, just in case Althea was inside, but she got no response. She thought she might leave a note, but she realized she hadn't brought paper and paper. "Maybe there's something to write with inside," she mumbled, knowing as she said it that she was making up excuses to check out the cottage. Still, she tested the doorknob. The door was unlocked.

It was instantly obvious to Maggie that Althea didn't enter the house this way often. Clutter covered the floor, and Maggie had to step carefully as she picked her way halfway across the room.

Maggie had heard that Althea kept sick and wounded animals out back and tried to nurse them to health. Maybe that's where Althea was.

She was almost back at the front door when she heard a roar from outside. She stepped onto the porch just as a Harley pulled up to the front steps. She walked closer to get a look at the rider, but all she could see was her own reflection in the visor that covered his face. Then the rider snatched off the helmet, and Maggie's mouth fell open.

"Althea?" the man said. "I'm looking for Cotton Wellford. He promised to build bookcases in the rental house for me. He said to catch him here." The man waited for a reply. When none came, he added, "Can you tell me where to find him?"

Maggie walked down the steps to stand next to the motorcycle. "You look just like the cover on your book," she said. "*Murder in the Afternoon*, right? I never thought I'd meet a best-selling author."

Paul Morgan gave Maggie a modest smile. "I'll be happy to sign the book for you," he said. "When will Cotton be back?"

"I'd better explain. I'm looking for Althea, too. I live down the road. I'm Maggie."

Paul nodded. "The interior designer. Cotton is working for you?"

"Not any more," Maggie answered, and her voice shook just a little. "Cotton was murdered yesterday. We found his body in the water near the Tabby Café." She watched the author's face closely, trying to judge his reaction. "Did you talk to him recently?"

"I was supposed to meet him yesterday at the café, but I got caught up in my work. I was in the middle of chapter three, and I wanted to keep going." A hint of regret crossed his face. "I wish now

38

I had met him. Maybe if he had been with me, he would have been all right. I guess he ended up in the wrong place at the wrong time." He shook his head sadly. "Why would anybody want to kill Cotton? What did he have that anybody could have wanted?"

Maggie ignored the question. "I was just heading back to my cottage. I'll come back later. Maybe Althea will be back by then."

Paul held out his helmet. "No need to walk. Let me give you a ride home."

Maggie hesitated for an instant, then took the helmet and pulled it on.

"Ever ridden on one of these babies?" Paul asked. Maggie shook her head. "You'll love it. Smooth as glass once you get going. How do we get to your house?"

Maggie gave him directions and climbed onto the cycle. She held onto him just a little tighter than necessary. The cycle breezed toward Maggie's house, and Maggie found she loved the ride. Racing down the dirt road, leaving a plume of dust in their wake, holding tightly around this handsome man's waist, Maggie found herself wishing she lived a lot farther away.

When Paul pulled into Maggie's yard, Possum growled, trying to look menacing. Then Maggie took off the helmet, and Possum ran to meet her. "You take your watchdog responsibilities seriously, don't you, girl?" Maggie said affectionately. Possum accepted a pat from Paul with good humor.

Paul brushed hair the color of winter marsh grass out of his eyes and looked around. "This is beautiful," he said. "You've done a wonderful job with your design. And the view is killer. Wish I had discovered Seaward before I started my first book. It's a writer's paradise—quiet and unspoiled. How did you get here?"

Maggie began to explain about house sitting for friends last year. They walked into the kitchen together, and Maggie finished the story while she made coffee. They carried their cups outside and settled into comfortable chairs on the front deck.

Paul took an appreciative sip. "How did you know I like coffee instead of tea or soda?" he asked.

Maggie laughed. "I just fixed what I like at this time of day," she said. "Amazing that you like coffee in the afternoon, too. A lot of people save it for the mornings."

"Sitting here with a lovely lady on a beautiful fall day certainly beats sitting at home in front of my computer by myself and thinking about murder," Paul said with a chuckle. "I haven't come up with a title for the book yet, but it's a sure bet it'll contain the word 'murder'. My agent says that word is the one mystery buffs always look for." Paul took another slow sip. "Say, this is good java."

"New Guinea Pea Berry. I have to order it. The pea berries are seeds that form inside the coffee berry. Makes for an interesting taste. I think it has a great fruity flavor, and it's perfect for the four o'clock slump."

"You'll have to order some for me," Paul remarked.

Maggie looked up in surprise. Until that second, she had not considered that he might want to see her again. *He doesn't know about John*, she thought, *but why should he?* She smiled as Paul talked softly about the novel he was working on. It had been a long time since she had enjoyed being around any man besides John. Maybe it was time that she explored her options.

Then she heard Paul say, "Don't you think?" and she realized she had no idea what he had asked. She felt her face go red. "I'm sorry," she stammered. "I was lost in thought."

"I said the Tabby Café has a wonderful menu, don't you think?" Paul gave her a warm smile. "Maybe you'd like to join me for dinner one day this week?"

This time, Maggie didn't stammer at all. "I'd like that. I need to check with my houseguest, but I suspect she'll be busy with Bill

Johnson. You know him, right? The top cop until the sheriff gets back? He and Hannah seem to be hitting it off quite well."

"They can join us," Paul answered. "I need to ask a professional about the victim I have dead on a street corner in chapter three anyway." Paul rose reluctantly. "Which reminds me—I'd better get back to work. I can't just leave corpses lying undiscovered on street corners, now can I?" He shot Maggie a devilish grin, and she noticed that his hazel eyes lit up when he smiled.

She watched until his motorcycle had roared out of sight.

She was still smiling when she walked back into the cottage. She rinsed the coffee cups and put them in the dishwasher. She was wondering whether it was too soon to go back to Althea's when she turned and found herself face to face with a man. She screamed and turned to run; then it dawned on her who he was.

"Bill," she wheezed, clutching her chest. "You almost scared me to death."

"You're awfully jumpy," Bill remarked. "I guess that's normal, considering what you and Hannah went through. Still, maybe you two ladies should move to the mainland until Cotton's killer is caught."

"Don't be absurd. I just didn't hear you and Hannah come in." Maggie dismissed the subject with a wave of her hand. "How was the Tabby today? Did I miss a delicious special?"

"The chef—whatever his name is—came out twice to look for you," Hannah said with a mischievous glint in her eye. "I think he's sweet on you, honey. That man makes an amazing key lime pie. He said he uses condensed milk, same as my granny used to. I'll gain at least five pounds if I keep going there. What do you say we go for a run tomorrow?"

Maggie nodded. "Let's do it early. That'll give us some energy for our presentation."

Hannah cleared her throat. "Uh…I was asking Bill if he wanted to run." She hesitated, then added reluctantly, "But I guess you could come, too, Maggie."

Maggie opened her mouth to decline, but Bill interrupted. "You ladies will have to go by yourselves," he said. "I'll be working. I'm expecting the preliminary autopsy results to come in tomorrow." Bill chewed his bottom lip. "I'll tell you, I don't think Cotton was killed at the dock. The scene's too clean. I think he was stabbed somewhere else and dumped there to throw us off." He looked up and saw, with distress, that he had Maggie's full attention. He waved his index finger at her sternly. "Now, look, just because I make an off-hand remark doesn't mean you can stick your nose in."

Maggie hardly heard the warning. "Maybe the killer was trying to make a point by dumping him at the Tabby's dock," she mused.

Bill sighed, whether in resignation at her sticking "her nose in" or just plain weariness, Maggie wasn't sure. "The Coast Guard is checking boats from here to Jacksonville. Robert had a list of the travelers that stopped for the night. If it was one of them, we'll know soon enough, I guess. Robert thinks Cotton may have run up on a stranger, maybe startled somebody out there at night, and they killed him, thinking he meant them harm, and then panicked. There are other theories floating around, too, but until we have more information, I don't think we can hazard a guess."

"I don't either," Maggie said. "We'll see what the autopsy results say."

Bill frowned but kept quiet. He turned to Hannah, and his face brightened. "Would you ladies like to join me for dinner after your Ribaut Inn presenta…"

"Yes!" Hannah answered before he could even complete the sentence. "We'll let you know what time we get through. Isn't there a new seafood place in Beaufort?"

"Or we could eat at the Inn," Bill suggested. "I've heard the food is always good there."

Maggie looked from one to the other and didn't say a word. But she couldn't help but smile.

"What's so funny?" Hannah demanded.

"Nothing at all," Maggie replied innocently. "Why don't we call Bill on his cell phone when the meeting with Chandler is over?"

Bill nodded and turned to leave. "I'm going to stop by Althea's on my way to Markley Marina," he said. "I know the Mary Grace will be late. It always is. See y'all tomorrow."

Hannah followed him out the door, and when she came back a few minutes later, she had a dreamy look on her face. "He's everything I've always wanted in a man," she gushed.

Maggie chuckled. "You say that about every new man you date."

"He's different," Hannah insisted. "He's strong and dependable, and he's thinking about moving down here permanently when Sheriff Hammond retires. You know he has a master's in law enforcement from Columbia University. He's no dummy."

A horrible thought occurred to Maggie. She turned to Hannah with a somber face. "You know, we really don't know anything about him, and Hammond wouldn't have bothered to check out his credentials. Bill seems like a nice enough guy, but so did Ted Bundy. What do we really know about him? He could be a disgraced cop, a desperate criminal who came here to hide out."

Hannah eyes flashed. "Don't be silly. He's one of the good guys, one of the heroes in a white hat. What's the matter with you?" Maggie opened her mouth to explain her reasoning, but Hannah had had enough of such talk. "Speaking of wearing a white hat," she said, "why don't you help me decide what to wear to the presentation? I want something nice, now, because we'll be meeting Bill later."

Maggie shook her head. "I'm meeting Salty George for another boat lesson. He's coming by my dock about five." She glanced at her watch. "It's almost five now. I've just got time to grab my windbreaker and change my shoes." Maggie gave Hannah a wave and dashed out to the deck to retrieve her boating shoes and the jacket she always wore. The shoes were right where she had left them, but her jacket was gone. "I must have left it on the boat last week," she muttered impatiently. She trotted off toward the dock.

Hannah stood on the deck and called after her, "You're crazy to get back in a boat after yesterday!"

Maggie kept moving. "If you fell off a horse, you'd get back on," she shouted over her shoulder. "Same principle."

Maggie broke into a run when she saw Salty George's boat glide up to her dock.

"We're going up to the ACE Basin this evening, at least as far as the Combahee," the captain told her when she had climbed aboard. Maggie knew that the three rivers—Ashepoo, Combahee, and Edisto—were part of a wildlife preserve, and it was the perfect time of day to spot wildlife.

"I'm going to show you how to anchor and turn the power off," Salty George told her. "Then you can get us back to Seaward."

Maggie took the helm. She loved the feel of the wheel in her hand and the salty breeze in her face. A boat was better than a convertible any day, Maggie decided.

The boat hit a two-foot wave, and Maggie felt a surge of elation as she held the boat steady.

Salty George had worked in the sun so long, his face was lined and leathery, but he was strong and quick. Maggie wondered how old he was: fifty or maybe even sixty? It was impossible to tell. Salty George didn't talk much, but he had told Maggie once that his wife didn't like boats, and she refused to accompany him on his charters to the Gulf. Maggie thought he appreciated having a student who understood his passion for the water.

"You still interested in your own little seaworthy vessel?" he called over the rumble of the engine. "I've found a Grady White for you. She's at the Beaufort marina. Man who owns her wants to go back North this winter. You can get a good deal. And the boat is just the right size for you. Can you come over to Beaufort to look at her?"

"Is Grady White the man who owns her?"

Salty George's mouth twitched, causing the lines in his face to deepen. But he managed not to laugh out loud. "Naw," he said. "It's the kind of boat. Like the Seaward Lady is a Boston Whaler. This Grady White has a closed bow, windshield, back-to-back seats that fold down to make a sun lounger. Even has room to store skis and life jackets under the main deck."

Maggie trusted his judgment. "I'd love to see it," she said.

Salty George reminded her, in some ways, of her father. Her father also loved the water. She remembered the first time he and a couple of his friends took her fishing on Lake Hartwell in the upstate. She had been eight or nine years old. The day had been bright and sunny, like this one. She could still hear the sound of her father's laughter and the pop-fizz of beer cans opening. She had learned to bait a hook that day. It had taken her most of the afternoon to work up the courage to touch the squirming worms. Her father had patiently convinced her to keep trying. Perhaps it was that day when she also learned never to give up on something that was really important. Her tenacity had been rewarded: She was the only one on the boat that day to catch a fish, and it had been a three-pound, large-mouth bass. Her father's friends had protested bitterly when she insisted on throwing it back.

Salty George's reprimand brought her back to the present. "Watch what you're doing!" he said sternly. "Keep your eye on the

GPS and slow down. Don't let your mind wander when you're captain of the boat." He frowned at her. "You been reading the boating book I loaned you?"

"I've read every word," she assured him. "It's easy to *read* about boating. Will I ever get the hang of it?"

His expression softened, though his voice remained gruff. "You're my best pupil," he said. He gave her one quick, hard pat on the back. It was the highest praise he had ever offered, and Maggie gave him a grateful smile. "When do you want to see the boat?" he asked.

"I have to be in Beaufort tomorrow afternoon for a meeting. Can you meet me?"

"I'm leaving early in the morning for the Gulf," he answered. "Taking some tourists from Hilton Head. Said they were from Arizona and want to do some fishing." He rubbed his scruffy chin, considering his timetable. "I should be back in the late afternoon." He nodded decisively. "I'll be there," he declared. "Call me on the cell when you're ready."

He hadn't mentioned the murder at all, Maggie realized, and she wondered if he had heard. Maybe he hadn't met Cotton, but a violent crime was big news on Seaward, no matter who the victim was. Salty George was a taciturn man by nature, though, and he probably didn't see any point in discussing the matter, Maggie thought. Still, she wanted to know if he had any theories.

"I guess you've heard what happened to my carpenter," she remarked. "Did you know Cotton Wellford?"

Salty George frowned and shook his head.

Maggie tried again. "Well, surely you heard what happened."

He ignored the question. "This is a good place to stop the boat," he said.

For another hour, he instructed Maggie in handling an anchor. He made her drop anchor twice and restart the engine. Then Maggie turned the boat around and headed back to her dock.

As they crossed the Intracoastal Waterway, they watched several sailboats float in the direction of Palmetto Bluff Marina and the Tabby Café. To Maggie's surprise, Salty George was in a mood for conversation. She suspected he might be testing her concentration, so she listened, but she kept her eyes on the water.

"I was born on the coast," he told her. "Always wanted to power a tug boat. Right up the Savannah River and into that beautiful port. Be the captain of my own tug. The wife never was interested in living on the water, though. Her thing is the flea markets. She likes to go to the one in Charleston every Saturday. Found some women who like to do the same thing, and she goes with them. She comes back with the damnedest junk." Maggie noted that his gruff tone softened ever so slightly whenever he mentioned his wife, Scotty. He nudged Maggie's arm. "We're almost at the dock," he said. "Want me to take her in?"

Maggie squared her shoulders. "Got to keep practicing," she said. "I want to have my own boat and take her from Seaward to the other islands. It's impossible to rely on the Mary Grace."

Maggie knew that docking was everything, and after her experience at Palmetto Bluff, she knew she had to force herself to keep her nerve. She knew she was coming in at high tide. She checked the wind and looked for traffic near the dock. She began to motor toward the pier at a thirty-degree angle, keeping the speed at idle. Salty George watched closely but kept his distance. She took the prop out of gear, turned the wheel away from the dock and let the momentum carry the stern toward her piling. She straightened the wheel and threw the engine into reverse. The boat stopped and floated sideways, just barely nudging the dock. Quickly, Maggie hopped out and got her bowline on the dock cleat. Leaving enough slack for the falling tide, she secured the stern.

She looked back and got an approving nod from Salty George. "I'll meet you tomorrow," he said. "Maybe the owner will let you have her for a day or two to see if you'd like to buy her. Your next assignment is a picnic on Sandibar Island. Only way to get there is by boat."

It was then that Maggie remembered her missing windbreaker. "Did I leave my jacket last week?" she called.

"Don't know. Look under the bow."

Maggie clambered back on board and looked around, but the jacket wasn't there. She did find something else under the bow, though, and it caused her to stumble backward. She took a minute to compose herself and went back for a closer look. There was no denying it: a large pool of dried blood—at least that's what it looked like.

Salty George spoke from just behind her, causing her to jump. "Did you find the jacket?" he asked.

She pointed shakily at the stain. "Is that blood?"

"Sure it is." Salty George said matter-of-factly. "That's what happens when you take tourists out to catch fish and they catch each other on the hooks instead. Or they cut up the fish when I'm not looking instead of waiting until they get back to shore. They make a damn mess all over the place." He shrugged. "What are you gonna do? It's how I make my living."

Maggie nodded, but her hands were shaking. "Well, I'll keep my eye out for your jacket," he continued. "I hope Scotty didn't find it and take it to a resale shop. She and that new friend of hers, Althea, are always scheming to make a buck."

Maggie's eyes widened at the mention of Althea's name, but she clamped her mouth shut. Better to keep her questions to herself, she decided, until she thought all this through. Maybe she would talk it over with Bill.

She waved to Salty George with a trembling hand and walked toward her cottage. She realized that he had not mentioned the murder at the Palmetto marina. If Scotty knew Althea, then Salty George must have known Cotton. Did fish blood look the same as human blood? Maggie had no idea. She shook her head impatiently. "Maggie, you have got to quit being so paranoid," she mumbled. "You better concentrate on your presentation at the Ribaut Inn, and while you're at it, you have to remember to ask Robert about renting the Seaward Lady for a picnic." She started writing a guest list for the picnic in her head: Bill and Hannah—and maybe Paul Morgan. Why not?

By the time she reached her door, she was smiling.

"Hey, Hannah, I'm home," she called. "Want to get dinner at the Red Eye?"

But the house was dark, and there was no response. Maggie flipped on the overhead light in the kitchen and found a note on the counter. She read it to Possum: "Bill missed the Mary Grace. Meet us at the saloon for dinner. Love ya, Hannah."

Possum showed no interest whatsoever. She was busy wrestling with a favorite toy, an elephant that squeaked when she squeezed it in her jaws.

Maggie tossed the note away. "Well, what do you think, Possum? Did Bill even try to catch the Mary Grace?"

Possum shook the elephant hard and raced out of the kitchen. Maggie could hear the toy squeak frantically as Possum bounced up the stairs to the bedrooms.

Maggie grabbed a sweater hanging in a hall closet and headed out the door. She didn't see the cardboard box that someone had left by the screen door until she stumbled over it. Her name was scribbled across the top, but there was no postmark. She didn't recognize the wobbly handwriting. It looked like a child might have written it, she thought. She sat on the stoop and ripped open the package.

At the top was a note that read: "Keep this until I get back. Cotton."

Tears sprang to her eyes. She dug into the box, expecting to find tools or work clothes. Instead, she found money, stacks of bills—twenties and fifties arranged in neat bundles.

Four

The Red Eye Saloon, once a seedy watering hole for Seaward Island's outcasts, had undergone a remarkable metamorphosis. It was now a soft gray clapboard building with steps painted to complement the Charleston green shutters on the sparkling windows. A sign over the front door sported a brightly colored blowfish whose red eye matched the Chinese red door. Maggie remembered a time when the grime on the windows was so thick, the brightest sunshine couldn't chase away the gloom inside the bar.

Maggie pushed opened the door and peered inside. Bill and Hannah had saved a seat for her at a table covered with a crisp red tablecloth.

Dickie, the owner, also had changed for the better. His long, greasy hair and dandruff-speckled glasses had been replaced by spotless wire-rims and a fashionable layered haircut. Maggie looked around the room, but she didn't see him. He must be out on a grocery run, she decided.

"What took you so long?" Hannah asked. "Bad boat lesson?" Hannah took a closer look at her friend. "Are you okay?"

Maggie took a deep breath. "I had a great lesson," she said. "Even plan to go to Sandibar by boat soon. You two want to go with me? We'll have a picnic. Maybe Thursday?"

Bill shook his head. "I have to work. There are some other crimes in this county besides the murder, and I'm not making much progress on Cotton's case. But, Hannah, you should go. Go early in the day and you won't run into thunderstorms."

"We ordered you a shrimp burger," Hannah told Maggie, "and some sweet potato fries. You don't need to pour catsup on them." Hannah wrinkled her nose. "Catsup has a lot of carbs, you know."

Maggie briefly considered telling Bill and Hannah about the new evidence she had turned up. She could let Bill check out the blood on Salty George's boat, and she probably should turn over Cotton's money. But she suppressed the impulse. For now, she wanted to ponder these things without interference.

Little Lavender sauntered up to the table, carrying shrimp-burger baskets. He had cleaned up, too, at Dickie's insistence, but no one could convince him to wear any color except purple. He had worn purple since he was a child; no one on the island could say why. Today he was resplendent in a purple checked chef's hat and a lilac smock. He set the baskets down and waited patiently for them to take a taste. Maggie understood this ritual of his, and she knew he wouldn't go away until they praised the food. Hannah and Bill, being newcomers, just dug in. Maggie saw a pout form on Lav's lower lip, and she took a quick bite. "My," she exclaimed, "this is the best I've ever eaten. Lav, your food just keeps getting better and better."

The pout was replaced by a proud smile. "I've made a new bisque," he proclaimed grandly. He looked around to make sure no one was looking and lowered his voice. "It's not on the menu, but for Maggie and her friends..." Lav had taken a cooking course at the tech college in Beaufort, and he was very proud of his newly acquired culinary skills.

"What kind of bisque?" Hannah asked, again showing her ignorance of the required ritual. But then she took a bite of the shrimp burger and gave Lav a thumbs-up, so he was pacified, and he let her little faux pas pass without comment.

"Cajun bean and shrimp," he answered. "I put onion, thyme, marjoram, and a little crushed pepper in it. You folks try it and tell me if I need to add corn and make it more like a chowder."

"Lav, that sounds amazing! You've turned into a real gourmet chef!" Maggie said with all the enthusiasm she could muster, sending Lav back into the kitchen with a big smile on his face.

Inevitably, the talk around the table turned to Cotton's murder. Maggie decided to keep her ears open and her mouth shut.

"Nothing has turned up from Seaward to Jax Beach, and it's not likely to," Bill remarked morosely. "I'll track down the ex-wife and Althea, and maybe I'll get some answers from them."

"Althea and Salty George's wife, Scotty, are friends," Maggie said, trying to sound casual. "Maybe you should check with them." *There, I've set him on the right path, maybe, but I haven't given away too much*, she thought, and her conscience quieted down.

Lav reappeared, carrying steaming bowls of bisque. He hovered anxiously until they had tasted his concoction and pronounced it delicious. When he finally walked away, Maggie wondered if Bill even remembered her remarks about Salty George and Scotty.

Bill swiped his napkin across his mouth and stood. "The Mary Grace should be here by now. Hannah, want to walk me to the dock?" He grabbed Hannah's hand, then he added with obvious reluctance, "What to come, Maggie?"

Maggie smiled and shook her head. "I'll stay and have another glass of Pinot Grigio."

Jim Hamilton, still wearing his white chef's smock, pushed through the front door as Bill and Hannah made their exit. He carried a tray of pastries and his locally famous key lime pie. He placed the tray on the bar, looked around the restaurant, and spotted Maggie. His face lit up, and he hurried to her table.

She motioned to an empty chair opposite her. "Join me," she said. "I've just had Lav's special, and I thought I'd just relax for a few minutes before I go back to the cottage. What are you doing here? Giving Lav lessons in dessert making?"

Jim chuckled. "The Red Eye buys a few desserts from us. I have a couple of hours off this time of day, then we get a rush about ten o'clock. I needed an excuse to get out of there for a while tonight anyway. Robert is going berserk trying to organize the wine-tasting. Thinks he has about eighty coming. He's been trying to reach you. He said maybe you could help him with the preparations. Everybody remembers what you did for this place with that festival last year."

Maggie nodded. "I'll call him tomorrow and see what I can do." She sighed and gazed out the window at the coral sky. "This is my favorite table," she said. "I can see the sunset from here."

A man wandered into the restaurant and held open the door for his female companion. On the breeze that followed them in, Maggie could hear a chorus of male tree frogs.

"Hear that?" she said with a laugh. "The tree frogs are the only live entertainment we have at the Red Eye. I like to think they're singing love songs, trying to attract the lady frogs."

"Well, that's the only mating call I'm likely to hear tonight," Jim remarked. His face reddened instantly, and he looked away.

Maggie laughed and gave his hand a comforting pat. When he turned back to face her, she noticed for the first time how his dark hair fell in curls over his right brow. And his eyes—why had she never noticed how green they were?

To ease his embarrassment, and to hide her own thoughts that had suddenly become unruly, she changed the subject. "You came here from the Santibel Grill in Georgetown?"

"I wanted to be closer to Savannah. I have a three-year-old there. Her mother, my ex, wants me to actually move to the city and take over a restaurant for her. I told Robert I'd stay here until Christmas at least. The Tabby already has a great reputation. Everything Robert does turns to gold. My gold goes to support my daughter. What about you?"

"I've never been married. I've been building my career as a designer." She didn't offer any information about the philandering man she had almost married, and she wasn't inclined to talk about John Heyward either.

Jim shifted nervously in his chair and cleared his throat several times. Finally, he blurted, "Want to go to Savannah Sunday? I have the day off, and we can see a movie or spend some time on Tybee. It's a great beach."

Maggie looked up in surprise; then she smiled. "Sounds great. Why don't you call me Saturday morning? Robert's got my number."

When Jim had gone, Maggie pondered her impulsive decision. This was a big step for her. Was she really ready to give up on John? She hadn't seen him in weeks, but still...

A booming voice interrupted her thoughts. Maggie looked up and saw Dickie charging toward her table. He turned a chair backwards and straddled it.

"Hope you're not trying to solve any murders these days, my friend," he said playfully. "You know, you almost got us killed the last time you tried that."

Maggie gave him a quick hug. "I was just talking to Jim," she said. "He brought in some desserts. He wants me to go to a movie with him." She eyed Dickie, waiting for his reaction. She had a lot of faith in Dickie's judgment.

Dickie rolled his eyes. "You mean Chef James Allen Hamilton the third. He seems a little stuck on hisself to me. Never has much to say when he comes in." Dickie shrugged. "Do what you want. I guess John's done been gone too long." Dickie leaned closer to Maggie with an urgent look on his face. "Listen, I need you to talk to Sallie, talk some sense into her head. She's gone and got the idea that my son has to be born on Seaward. Says I was and he should be, too. Granny Jones is the only midwife left on this island, and she's getting mighty old. I think Sallie should stay on the mainland and have the baby at Baptist General. They got equipment if anything goes wrong." Dickie shot Maggie a beseeching look. "Will you talk some sense into her? If Sallie stays here, her mama will be over at my garage every day tryin' to fix the place up with curtains and all that fancy stuff. You know Toot won't stand for that."

"How is the garage doing?" Maggie asked, adeptly sidestepping the plea for help.

"Toot's turned out to be a real good mechanic. The place ain't making money yet, but it will soon enough. I really 'preciate that investment in the place, Maggie. You won't regret it."

Maggie waved away his thanks. "It was a sound business investment."

"What about Sallie Jo? Will you talk to her? You know we can't afford to lose our only mechanic, and we will, sure as hell, if Sallie's mama tries to put up frills and lace in that garage."

Maggie pictured big, tough, greasy Toot adjusting a carburetor amid pink ruffles, and she had to laugh. "I'll talk to her. Maybe I can bribe her with a baby shower."

Maggie wondered how she would broach the subject that was really on her mind.

"Say, Dickie, what's the gossip on the island about Cotton's death?"

Dickie frowned. "What are you up to?"

Maggie arranged her face into an expression of injured innocence. "I'm just curious, like everybody else."

Dickie stared into her eyes for a minute, trying to judge her intent. "Well, most of this side of the island hopes it was a tourist passin' through on a boat. We got more people over here than we used to have. We just don't know the background of the locals like we used to. I heard the Meyers house was for sale. Did they move to Aspen?"

"Yes, but no one's bought it yet. Some change is good for Seaward."

Dickie set his mouth belligerently. "Just better not build one of them giant malls over here. Some guy named Chandler is building something big in Savannah. And he's bought the Inn in Beaufort."

"That's not a bad thing, Dickie," Maggie assured him. "I may get my first job from him. Hannah and I hope to redo the cottages behind Ribaut Inn. If it works out, I'll have the beginning of my design firm, and I won't have to do any more work for Rodale's firm in Charleston."

Maggie reached into her purse and tossed some bills on the table. "I'll run over to Sallie's before I go home," she said. "I haven't seen her for a while, anyway, and I've missed her. You leaving soon?"

Dickie shook his head. "I promised Lav I'd close tonight." He waggled his eyebrows suggestively. "I think he's got a hot date. Watch out for wild boars. They out and roaming this time of year. Tell Sallie I'll try to be home by midnight, okay?" Maggie turned to leave, but Dickie called her back. "By the way, I met your friend Hannah. She was gittin' on the Mary Grace with Bill when we got off. Left you a note, she said. Something about wanting to get the feel of the Inn before you make the presentation."

"That's not what she wants to get the feel of," Maggie muttered.

Dickie just looked puzzled. "Huh?"

"Never mind." She gave him a quick wave. "See you later," she called over her shoulder as she pushed through the door.

The locals had named their own streets, and the road to Dickie's house was named Tree Toad Lane. Maggie had asked someone about Ruthless Lane down by the Kash and Karry. Harry, the clerk who worked the register, told her that a woman named Ruth had run away with a man selling sno-cones, and her husband had renamed the road. Harry couldn't say whether the husband was celebrating her departure or mourning. Remembering the story,

Maggie chuckled to herself. Seaward was the most original place Maggie had ever lived.

Maggie's stroll took her to the Diamonds' log cabin in just a few minutes. She walked up the front steps and was greeted from the porch by Sallie Jo, Sallie's mother, Inez, and Bobby Lymon, a local who had made his living shrimping out of Jenkins Creek since he was twelve years old. He had parked his fisherman's boots on the steps, and his bare feet were propped on a paisley ottoman.

Sallie Jo led Maggie inside the house. It was furnished with painted pieces handed down several generations. Maggie had given Sallie scraps from her Scalamandre yardage, and Sallie and her mother had sewed slipcovers and curtains with the material. Maggie was always amazed at the resourcefulness of the island women. They didn't waste a thing. Even bacon drippings were saved in tin cans on just about every stovetop on Seaward.

Sallie had pink plastic curlers in her hair. Nearly every time Maggie saw Sallie, those curlers covered her head. Maggie always wondered how anyone could sleep in those things. Before she came to Seaward, Maggie had blown her long, blond hair dry every morning. Now she was content to let it air dry into natural waves.

Tonight, Sallie looked happy, and she gave Maggie a hug as she ushered her in.

"You've come to make me go back to the mainland," Sallie remarked before Maggie could utter a word. "You can save your breath. I've decided to have Junior in the hospital, but Dickie is drivin' me crazy; he's over anxious. It's six weeks until this baby pops out. Doc says he's gonna weigh at least nine pounds. I got plenty of time to go to the mainland, and there's lots to do. Mama and me finished the nursery in that blue cloth you gave us. Made a pretty crib cover. And Toot painted the walls—a seascape. Just the palest green, like you suggested." Sallie Jo sighed contentedly. "It's so, so beautiful."

She waddled to the couch and sat down carefully, holding her stomach.

Bobby had followed the women inside, and he waited for Sallie Jo to take a breath. He leaned against a wall, his arms crossed, and watched Maggie. Clearly, he had something on his mind. "That new sheriff gonna do something about them foreign shrimpers?" he asked. "Most of them're breaking the law and not giving me a chance to get my catch."

"Are you talking about the foreign imports? Our legislature has to do something about that. There are trade issues involved."

Bobby gave her a blank stare. "All I know is the 'fruit of the sea' ain't coming from my boat. If I get a good catch, most of the restaurants won't buy."

"Talk to Robert Davis," Maggie suggested. "He'll buy shrimp from you and other locals, too. I'll tell him to look out for you. You go over to the Tabby Café and ask for him."

Bobby grunted, unconvinced. "You mean that big shot would talk to somebody like me?"

"He's a great guy," Maggie answered. "He's always ready to support the locals. He'd rather buy from you. Maybe he'd help you form a co-op and get the local shrimpers into other restaurants in the area. Our shrimp tastes much better than the imported."

Sallie Jo sniffed with disdain. "That imported trash has been frozen," she said. "I can always tell the difference. Lav only uses the catch from Bobby for our specials at the Red Eye. You sure Mr. Davis would be interested? His chef didn't seem to be when Lav talked to him."

"I don't think he has the authority to buy. Robert does that. I'll straighten it out," Maggie assured them. Sallie Jo smiled and relaxed in her chair, knowing that Maggie would keep her promise. Hadn't she helped organize the festival last year that had enabled her and Dickie to renovate the Red Eye? The locals often called on

Maggie for her help, and Maggie was always generous with her time and ideas.

Bobby retrieved his boots and pulled them on slowly. "Thanks," he called to Maggie through the screen door as he left.

Inez had fallen asleep in her recliner, and the television played softly in the background. Sallie Jo motioned for Maggie to follow her onto the porch. Maggie had convinced Sallie Jo to keep the metal chairs that were pushed up against the house. A fresh coat of white paint and new pink cushions had made them attractive and comfortable. Sallie had seen the same chairs for seventy-five dollars at a yard sale on the mainland, and she had confided to Maggie that she would have been very upset had she thrown her own away.

Sallie Jo eased herself into one of them and Maggie took the other. The two women always enjoyed sharing the news around the island, but tonight, when the conversation turned to Cotton's murder, Sallie Jo pointed a stern finger at Maggie. "Don't get Dickie involved in that mess," she commanded. "You almost got him killed last year when they found that dead student and you talked him into nosing around with you."

Maggie smiled to reassure her friend. "I'm minding my own business this time—literally. Hannah and I are doing a presentation, and if we get the job, I'll be busy for months. Anyway, I'm not sure Cotton's murderer is a local. Maybe it was just someone who happened to run into him on our island."

Sallie Jo's eyes widened. "Not local?" she almost shouted. "Who do you think Cotton was? He was from the only family that has been here since the early forties. They come over to sharecrop and stayed. Cotton was born here, and how do you think he got his name? His daddy grew cotton, and when he was born with blond hair, they named him Cotton. Bobby and him have been having a feud about the shrimp for years, and I figure maybe Cotton was feuding with other local shrimpers, too. Cotton thought it was okay to bait the waters, and some of the shrimpers hated it. How come you don't know this?"

Maggie shrugged. "Cotton didn't live on the island; I just figured he came from somewhere else."

"He married that tramp Delores, and she took him away," Sallie Jo huffed. "Think he was moving back after his divorce. Reckon Althea is heartbroken. She was his sweetheart, you know. I'm going over to see her tomorrow."

"I looked for her today, but I couldn't find her," Maggie said.

"She mighta been at the funeral home. She'd be in charge now."

Maggie stretched wearily and stood up. "It's been a long day," she said. "I need to get a good night's sleep. I want to throw you a baby shower in the next couple of weeks. Can you give me a list of people you want to invite by the weekend?"

Sallie Jo and Maggie parted with a hug. Maggie turned on the penlight she always carried and started back down the road to her own cottage.

The island sky reminded Maggie of black velvet. Humidity made the air feel heavy and caused fog to swirl around her feet. Maggie stepped carefully, but her mind was racing. There was an island connection for Cotton. Maggie knew that Cotton had wanted her to keep the money safe. She would hide it until Bill had a suspect. She wasn't convinced that the money had anything to do with the murder anyway. A lot of locals didn't trust banks on the mainland. This could have been Cotton's life savings, and he knew Maggie could be trusted with it.

Maggie passed the Red Eye, deep in thought. She noticed a light in the kitchen. Dickie was still cleaning up, she thought with a smile. She walked farther down the road, and as the light from the restaurant faded, she hurried her steps; she had never liked this dark stretch of road. And then she heard something that sounded like an echo of her footsteps. She stopped and listened. Nothing.

"Anyone there?" she called. Only the tree frogs answered her.

She heard a door slam in the distance and decided Dickie must finally be headed home. Then she heard footsteps crunching across oyster shells in Dickie's parking lot.

Whoever was behind her was walking on the dirt road now— walking quickly.

She began to run. The illumination from her penlight bounced crazily along the dusty road. She made it to her gate in record time.

Possum greeted her with doggie kisses and tail wagging. Maggie leaned down to pet her.

"Possum, I have a vivid imagination," she complained.

She opened the door, and she and Possum walked inside.

She didn't see the shadowy figure that passed silently by her gate, stood for a moment staring at her cottage, and then turned and walked back toward the interior of the island.

Five

Maggie awoke with the anticipation of an important day in front of her. She and Hannah had talked on the phone at least three times, and Maggie had modified their presentation plan. Hannah had done an overall view of the Inn and thought their main plan looked great. She had told Maggie she would do some shopping, meet Bill for lunch, and be in the lobby of the Inn before five o'clock.

Maggie and Hannah had decided against dressing casually for the presentation, and Maggie was studying her outfit in the mirror when she heard a loud knock at the door facing the water.

"Anyone here?" Robert called.

"I'll be down in a minute," she shouted back.

Robert was sitting on the porch when Maggie came down. She had chosen a black skirt and an emerald blazer. The blazer conveyed that she meant business, but it wasn't as serious as if it were black like the skirt.

Robert gave Maggie an admiring look. "Hey, gorgeous," he said. "You must be working today. Got time for me?"

"Always," she answered, taking a seat opposite him at the kitchen table. "I wanted to talk to you about the local shrimpers anyway. Won't you consider buying from the locals for the restaurant?"

Robert grinned. "I tell you what: If you'll give Jim Hamilton a hand with my wine-tasting, I'll buy my shrimp from Bobby and his boys. I'm inviting the whole island, and I've faxed an invitation to all the marinas in North Carolina and Virginia. Lots of snowbirds should show up. Jim's a great chef, but he's not as good at planning as I had hoped."

Maggie nodded enthusiastically. "That would be great. It'll give me an excuse to see more of him. You know, Robert, I'm tired of sitting in this cottage alone. It's time for me to start dating again."

Robert gave Maggie a thumbs-up. "Glad to hear it," he said. "From the way John talks when he calls from Montana, he's in no hurry to get home. I think he really likes it there."

Maggie felt a lump rise in her throat, but she was determined not to let John or anyone else upset her on this important day. To change the subject, she asked, "Have things calmed down at the café? I hope your business hasn't been hurt by Cotton's death."

"It's even better," Robert exclaimed. "Isn't that awful? People are passing the marinas in Beaufort and Savannah to come to my place."

"Salty George wants me to look at a boat this afternoon in Beaufort, but I'm a little worried about meeting him." Maggie leaned over and added in a confidential whisper, "I saw blood in his boat yesterday, and it made me nervous."

Robert threw back his head and guffawed. "Fish gore," he said, wiping tears of mirth out of his eyes. "His boat is always a wreck. Don't get paranoid on me now and start seeing murderers around every bend. Bill Johnson is a smart man. He'll figure it out."

"If Hannah will leave him alone for at least a few minutes," Maggie retorted. "She acts like they're in love and they've only known each other a couple of days. I don't have to provide entertainment for her, at least. Bill seems to be doing that for me."

"I'll tell you what," Robert said. "I'll have my mechanic at Palmetto Bluff take a look at that boat Salty George wants to show you."

"I know I'm forgetting to ask you something, but I've got to run to catch the Mary Grace," Maggie said. "Something weird is going on. Randy and Dianne are always late early in the morning and on their last run at night. The rest of the day usually runs smoothly, though. When I have my own boat, I won't depend on their whims."

Robert stood slowly, and Maggie saw that he looked a little glum. He had told her once that he loved the way she had redone his house, but he hated that it was usually empty. She surmised from that remark that he was often lonely, and she could tell he was reluctant to leave her company. She made a mental note to make more of an effort to spend time with him.

Maggie walked to the dock at Markley Marina and saw that the Mary Grace was pulling into her berth right on schedule. She waited for a few locals to disembark and jumped aboard. Jim bounded up the gangplank right behind her.

"It's a beautiful day for a trip to the mainland," he noted with a grin. "I'm headed in for supplies for the restaurant, and I was delighted to see that you would be accompanying me over."

"I'm happy to see you, too," Maggie answered with a warm smile.

"Want to have dinner in town? We can talk about the wine-tasting. Robert said he was going to get you to help out, no matter what it took."

"He twisted my arm," Maggie said with a playful roll of her eyes. "I'd be glad to have dinner with you, but Bill and Hannah will have to be invited, too. She and I have a meeting in town this afternoon."

"Why don't we meet at six-thirty at the Baja Grill? They always have good food."

The ferry pulled into the Beaufort marina more than ten minutes early, cutting short the conversation. For once, Maggie wished the Mary Grace had lagged a little.

As she climbed the steps leading away from the ferry, Maggie noticed the Mary Grace was leaving already. According to the schedule, it should have stayed in port for twenty minutes. It was time for a little talk with Dianne and Randy on her ride back tonight, she decided. The young couple was inconveniencing a lot of people who depended on that ferry to take them to and from the mainland.

Maggie strolled down the dock, looking for Salty George. He waved to her from a boat she had never seen before. She ran toward it and fell in love at that very moment. A sixteen-foot Grady White! She had never cared so much for an inanimate object. She knew instantly she had to own this boat. She could picture herself powering it through the rough waves of the Atlantic.

She hopped aboard and looked around in awe. The boat was clean and perfect for a runabout. She could take it from Beaufort to Seaward and lots of other islands along the way. "Tell me about her," Maggie said. "Why is she being sold?"

"The owner is buying a bigger fishing boat," Salty George answered. "Wants to take himself out to the Gulf instead of paying me all the time. I'd just as soon have it that way. He's my wife's cousin and always wants a free ride. Got time for a little spin in the Beaufort River?"

"May I take her?" Maggie asked eagerly. "Does she have a name?" Maggie turned the key and felt the Yamaha jump to life. She steered toward open water, peppering Salty George with questions. "Did he say what his asking price is? I want Robert to look at her for me, too. How soon do I have to let you know if I can buy it? At the moment, I'm having a cash flow problem." Maggie took a breath and smiled at Salty George.

"You'll have Cash Floe if you buy her," he replied.

"What?"

"That's the boat's name: Cash Floe. F-l-o-e."

Maggie burst out laughing. "Perfect. She's easy to handle. Already feels like mine. I'll let you know later this week." She turned the boat and headed back to the marina.

Salty George pointed to something in the distance. "Would you look at that? The Mary Grace is way off course. Ain't she supposed to be going back to Seaward for her next run? Looks like she's going to Savannah. That young couple ain't making money if they keep getting off course." He scratched his head. "Glad I don't have to depend on them to get me to work."

Maggie agreed. She made a mental note to ask Dianne where the ferry was headed. It was almost time for her meeting at the Inn; otherwise, she would have chased them down.

After docking the boat by herself and accepting praise from Salty George, she headed toward the Ribaut Inn. How silly, she chided herself, to have believed that Salty George could have killed someone. He was a great guy, and he had helped her find just the right boat. She dug her cell phone out of a pocket and called Robert. By the time she had asked him to get his mechanic over to check out the boat, she had reached the lobby of the Inn.

Hannah was waiting for her. "The lobby pictures are wonderful," Hannah gushed. "Local artists depicting different aspects of the Sea Islands."

Maggie walked to the front desk and told the clerk that Chandler Morris was expecting them. She and Hannah fidgeted nervously on a sofa facing a mural that explained how the Inn was named. Chandler had told her the story at their first meeting.

"Want to hear the story of the French influence in South Carolina?" Maggie asked.

Hannah had her silver compact out to check her flawless face. "I'm listening," she said.

Maggie leaned against the burgundy camel back sofa. "A group of Huguenots," she began, "French Protestants with a man named Ribaut, sailed to this shore around May of maybe 1562. A fort was built on the waters of Port Royal. The region was named Carolus or something close. It honored King Charles IX of France. Ribaut returned to France and left settlers behind, but they gave up, built a boat, and left. An eighteen-year-old stayed behind and married an Indian princess."

"Does half of the lowcountry claim to be descendants of the marriage?" Hannah asked.

"There's a town up the road named Ruffin. That was the adventuresome lad's name."

Maggie and Hannah were giggling over the story when Sherman Pritchard swept down a hall that led to Chandler's office and into the lobby. "What's so funny?" he asked. "Is it fit to print?"

Maggie took in his perfectly pressed seersucker suit and perfectly knotted red-plaid bowtie. He oozed Southern gentleman charm. Maggie had heard that his mother had moved from Charleston and married a professor of literature at the university of Connecticut. Sherman was born there, and he didn't move to the lowcountry until his father bought the *Seaward Times* a few years ago. The *Times* had started its life as a penny coupon tabloid, and Sherm Senior had tried to bring credibility and class to his paper. Maggie wasn't sure, now that Senior had died, what Junior planned to do with the paper. But he damn sure wasn't going to bring it credibility and class.

"Has Bill received the autopsy report?" Sherman asked Hannah. "Will that tell us if the murder was premeditated?"

Hannah opened her mouth to answer, but Maggie grabbed her by the arm and hauled her toward the ladies' room. "We'll talk to you later," she called as she opened the door and shoved Hannah inside.

Hannah looked astounded and a little angry.

"Don't say a word to any reporter," Maggie warned. "You might give something away that Bill doesn't want the killer to know."

"I was just going to tell him that we didn't have an autopsy report yet, and he could check with Bill. I know I'm not supposed to tell anyone that Cotton may have been murdered the night before and frozen before he was moved. The time of death may be off."

This was news to Maggie. Before she could reply, a toilet flushed, and the two women went silent. A tall, redheaded stranger walked to the sink to wash her hands. She left the restroom without a word.

"I hope that woman was a tourist and not a local," Maggie said. "Bill will be furious if he finds out that you've been repeating what he told you in confidence. We won't be able to discuss the case at dinner, by the way. Jim Hamilton is joining us."

Hannah didn't seem the least bit worried that she might have spilled some pretty important beans. "He's adorable," she gushed. "And I love the way he looks at you. He's got great potential."

The door to the bathroom swung open, and Chandler Morris' assistant called to them. "We're waiting," she said.

Not a great way to begin a presentation, Maggie thought. Sherman wasn't anywhere in sight as they walked through the lobby and into a conference room.

After introductions, Maggie began by opening her worn leather bag. It had been a present from her mother when she graduated from design school. She always carried her storyboards to a presentation in it.

She took a deep breath and plunged in.

"I'll begin today by presenting the concept that Hannah and I think will fit into your renovated cottages. Jackson Downing in 1848 tried to influence his clients to keep their dwellings unpretentious. A simple, clean line in cottage style follows this philosophy. Cottage furnishings are crafted from indigenous materials in harmony with their surroundings. The concepts we are presenting today offer an ambiance that suits the lifestyle of the lowcountry." Maggie took a calming breath. She could tell she had caught Chandler's attention. He quit fiddling with his coffee cup and listened carefully. She continued the presentation with help from Hannah, who elaborated on the details of the theme in each of the three cottages.

69

"Our final room," Hannah said, "in our lowcountry cottage theme is the palmetto. The palmetto is the state tree in South Carolina and fits into the environment of the Inn, surrounded by sea oats and marshy sea grass. For those of you not native to this state, the palmetto became the state's symbol from a Revolutionary War battle at Fort Moultrie. This dates back to around June of 1776. The protection from palmetto trees allowed General William Moultrie to gain his victory over the British Redcoats. The British could not dominate or capture this part of the coast. General Moultrie put the tree on his regiment flag, and later it was put on the state flag.

"People visiting this area want to celebrate this unique history. This room—the Palmetto Room—gives them the chance to enjoy the beauty of the area and understand its history. The palmetto cottage overlooks the Beaufort River. We plan to use the teals and blues of this water backdrop in our fabrics."

When the presentation was over, there was a brief silence followed by applause. Chandler hired them on the spot. They agreed on a tentative timeline and a cost estimate based on their choice of fabrics and other materials. "There's just one hitch," Chandler said. "I've been out of town, and I haven't been able to get hold of my carpenter, Cotton, since I got back."

The room went silent.

Maggie thought she had seen Sherman coming out of Chandler's office. Surely Chandler knew about the murder. If not, it wasn't her place to tell him. Even Hannah kept silent, a rare occurrence. Maggie and Hannah shook hands with Chandler and walked out of the conference room, down the hall, and out the lobby door.

"How could he possibly not know?" Maggie whispered when they were a safe distance from the Inn.

"I think Bill needs to talk to that man," Hannah answered. "He was hiding something with that innocent remark about not being able to find Cotton. Do we really want to work for him?"

"Hey, we don't know that he was hiding anything," Maggie shot back. "I don't know about you, but I need the money. I found my boat today, and I intend to buy it if Robert's mechanic gives me the go-ahead."

Hannah bounced up and down and clapped her hands. "How exciting! Maybe we can take her for a ride this week."

"I'll try to set it up so we can take her on the picnic to Sandibar Island. Salty George wants me to practice throwing the anchor. He says I should go on a few short trips before I try to take a boat from Seaward to the Beaufort marina."

When the two friends arrived at the Baja, their dates were waiting for them at a table on a screened-in porch. They were sipping beers and arguing about the Braves.

"How did it go?" they both asked at once.

Hannah started talking about the presentation, and Maggie knew it would be a while before she hushed. Maggie ordered a glass of Shiraz and waited. There was nothing like a glass of wine to help her unwind after a successful presentation. Everyone agreed that the chef at their table should order for them. The waitress, a chubby, thirty-something brunette, flirted with Jim, and he responded by inviting her to eat at the Tabby Café sometime. Maggie watched the interplay and decided she didn't mind.

But she did mind when Hannah started yakking about Chandler's remarks after the presentation. She kicked Hannah under the table. Hadn't she told Hannah no more than a couple of hours ago that they couldn't discuss the case in front of Jim? But Hannah paid no attention, and Bill didn't seem upset, either.

Hannah concluded her recitation of events breathlessly and waited for Bill's reaction. When he didn't speak, she asked, "Well? Do you think Chandler had anything to do with Cotton's murder?"

Bill shrugged. "I've got several leads I'm working on. I'll get one of the deputies to go by and talk to him. I doubt he has any connection, though. Let's not make a big deal out of it. If there's nothing to it, then we haven't smeared the man's name all over town."

"What kind of leads?" Jim asked. "Is there anything we need to know or look out for at the café?"

Bill looked around the table, then held up his hands in a gesture of surrender. "Look, I'm going to let Sheriff Hammond take care of this thing. I talked to him this afternoon." Bill ignored the general air of disappointment in response to his announcement and grinned at Maggie. "He said to tell Maggie to stay out of it."

Maggie felt her face go red, and she giggled. "Is he catching any fish or just telling lies about it?"

It was getting dark when they left the restaurant. On the walk back to the marina, Bill and Hannah dropped behind. They seemed in no hurry to get Hannah on the boat. Maggie explained the sheriff's warning—and the trouble she had gotten into last year—to Jim as they strolled.

"You must be a good detective," he said. "Robert predicted you would find the killer before Bill does."

"Oh, no," Maggie answered firmly. "Not this time. I'm staying out of it. And, anyway, I don't have a clue. Everybody liked Cotton."

"I wish I had known him. Everybody has great things to say about him." Jim stopped walking and looked back in the direction they had come. "Oh, no, I left my jacket back at the restaurant. The Mary Grace isn't here yet. I probably have time to run back and get it."

He raced away, and Maggie watched him go. He was such a nice guy, but what about that flirting with the waitress right under Maggie's nose? Maybe he didn't consider the dinner a real date. Maybe he just wasn't interested in a real relationship.

Hannah announced she needed to find the marina's restroom. *She wants to fix her hair again*, Maggie thought. Bill wandered off to say hello to Shinder Booze, the day man at the reception desk at the Dew Drop Inn on the other side of the bridge. He was a great source for country gossip, and Maggie knew Bill wanted to get to know him. She walked alone to the edge of the dock. A sliver of light shone on the horizon, probably the Mary Grace chugging toward the marina—late again. Next week, everybody would set their clocks back an hour, and the days would grow even shorter.

Maggie spotted a familiar sixteen-foot dinghy tied up at the dock. The Turners had come back for another visit.

Gulls screeched just overhead, and Maggie watched them circle. She heard footsteps behind her and thought Jim was returning, but she kept her eyes on the gulls. She felt a pair of strong hands shove her from behind. She stumbled and lost her balance. Just before she fell into the water, she smelled a familiar aroma. Citrus. Limes, maybe. Or was it more flowery?

Her head slammed against the dinghy as she hit the water.

Six

Cold salt water flooded Maggie's nose and mouth. She panicked, flailing until she managed to surface. She coughed and gagged and finally gasped air into her lungs. She tried to grab an algae-covered piling and thought she saw a hand reaching toward her. She wasn't sure if the person reaching for her wanted to save her or finish her off. Then someone grabbed her hand and lifted her to safety. She saw Paul Morgan's face, and she collapsed against him, still gasping for air. He held her tightly.

"Isn't it a little late in the season for a swim?" His tone was light, but his eyes showed concern.

"Did you see who pushed me?" Maggie demanded through chattering teeth. "Someone shoved me. I think he meant for me to drown."

"Are you sure you didn't just get too close to the edge and fall in? I didn't see anyone, but I was in the marina store when I heard you scream."

She looked up at Paul in surprise. "I didn't realize I yelled."

She looked around, still in a daze. The Mary Grace had arrived, and a group of passengers was disembarking while people headed back to Seaward were beginning to form a line to get onboard. She realized there was no way to identify the man—or woman—who pushed her. She heard the gulls again, but this time they sounded as though they were laughing. Paul kept his arms around her as he led her off the dock. Bill and Hannah were suddenly at her side, shouting questions. Maggie heard Jim's voice, too. He sounded frightened.

Sherm Pritchard raced around a corner and ran in her direction, shouting questions.

"What's going on?" he said, puffing from the exertion. "I'm always the last to hear the news."

No one laughed.

"Apparently, somebody pushed Maggie into the river," Paul said. "Help me get her to the Mary Grace."

"Shouldn't we get her to a doctor?" Hannah asked.

Maggie shook her head. "No doctor," she said. "I'm all right. I just want to go home."

Paul and Bill held onto Maggie's arms while Hannah and Jim trailed behind. They helped Maggie find an empty bench on the ferry just before its engines started. Someone found her a blanket as the ferry began to move toward Seaward. The blanket smelled like old taco salad, but she clung to it and tried to stop shivering.

Paul sat at Maggie's side and rubbed her arms to warm her up. Jim sat on the other side and held her hand. "Are you okay?" he asked.

Bill stood over her, looking grim. "Can you tell me what happened?" He held a notebook and pen, ready to take down her answers.

So did Sherm.

"I didn't see anything," Maggie answered. "I felt a shove, and I fell into the river. I didn't hear anything either, except some footsteps behind me."

Bill glanced at Sherm, looking annoyed. "Take it easy," he told Maggie. "We'll talk later."

Hannah leaned over to hug Maggie. She wrinkled her nose. "Phooey, that smells like dried Mexican cumin that's rotted in the sun. Aren't these ferry owners supposed to keep things clean?"

"I don't care about that," Maggie snapped. "I'm sore, wet, cold, and furious. If someone pushed me in as a joke, they better tell me now—before I find out on my own."

She glared at each person around her in turn. No one spoke.

"Oh, God," she groaned. "Did I drop my bag in the water? Are the plans for the Inn ruined?"

"It's here," Hannah told her. "It was on the dock. You must have set it down or dropped it before you fell."

Maggie rifled through the bag, taking stock. "I can't find my phone," she remarked. But, under the circumstances, a missing phone was hardly a big deal.

When the ferry docked at Markley Marina, Jim took her arm and led her off the boat. Paul stayed close behind, and Bill and Hannah followed. Sherm Pritchard stayed onboard. Jim found a friend's golf cart parked nearby and helped Maggie onto the passenger seat. He drove toward her cottage, with the others, also in golf carts, trailing behind.

Possum barked a greeting as the parade of carts parked by the gate. Maggie's yard started to resemble the back nine at the Beaufort Golf Club. She sighed, knowing it would be a long night.

"I'll call Sprint in the morning," Hannah called as she climbed out of her cart. "You can probably pick up a new phone the next time you're in town."

She and Maggie walked slowly to the back door. As soon as they opened it, they stiffened in alarm. They could hear a man shouting, and then a deafening chorus of voices. It was only when they heard someone crooning "Singing in the Rain" that they realized the plasma TV was playing full blast.

Maggie groaned. "It's Granny Jones," she told Hannah. "She must be in the den. She loves that movie, and she won't leave until it's over."

Everyone trooped into the den, and, indeed, Granny Jones was seated on the love seat, a big smile on her face.

"I didn't know you had a TV in here," Hannah said.

Granny cackled. "Watch this," she said.

She turned off the TV, pushed a button on the remote control, and the credenza opened. Another click, and the TV disappeared into the opening, which closed behind it. Granny slapped her knee and cackled again. "Now, don't that beat all?"

"I designed it, and Cotton built it for me," Maggie explained. "He was the best."

"God rest his soul," Granny added somberly, looking toward heaven.

Maggie collapsed on the sofa, gingerly rubbing the knot on her head, and Hannah went into the kitchen for drinks and snacks. Jim sat down quickly at Maggie's side, and Paul moved to the other end of the sofa. Possum sniffed at Paul curiously and offered her paw. Paul gave her a friendly pat. "She's a beautiful Lab," he said.

Granny squirmed in her seat and stared at Maggie. She was upset about something, Maggie could tell, and she wouldn't wait much longer to get it off her chest.

"I'm exhausted, Granny," Maggie said gently. "Can't it wait until morning?"

Granny set her jaw. "No, ma'am, it most certainly cannot," she said with an accent that was undeniably lowcountry. "It's 'bout Albert, the pig."

Granny had lived in the lowcountry all her life. Most of her family had moved to the mainland long ago, but Granny wasn't going to leave her home. She was the only island resident who didn't evacuate when Hurricane Hugo blew through in 1989. A reporter asked her what it had been like to weather a hurricane alone. Her only comment had been: "Blast it! My roses done been pulled out of the ground."

When Hannah began to pass out food and drinks, Maggie slipped away for a shower. Maybe Granny would give up and go away while she was gone.

She should have known better. Granny had a captive audience. She was telling a story, gesturing wildly, when Maggie walked back into the den. It was the one about Bobbie Jefferson and his brother Kenny going on a coon hunt and getting lost. Maggie had heard it three times.

Granny's story ended just as Maggie sat down between Jim and Paul. Hannah and Bill were sprawled on the floor, sipping Shiraz.

"Are you sure you didn't see or hear anything before you were pushed?" Bill asked. "Did you actually feel a shove when you went off the dock? No one was around when the Mary Grace pulled in."

"I was pushed," Maggie said firmly. "Let's not make a big deal out of it. Maybe it was somebody's idea of a prank. I'll just keep my eyes open and see what happens."

Before Bill could respond, Jim and Paul had gallantly offered to keep an eye out for strangers on Seaward.

"It has to be someone we don't know," Hannah said with certainty. "Maybe someone who wants to know what you and Cotton talked about when he worked here."

Granny cleared her throat to speak, and everyone else got quiet. When Granny had something to say, you just sat back and listened. You didn't have much choice.

"My nephew and the twins, Bea and Beau, tol' me Althea is gonna sell Albert."

"Albert?" Hannah interrupted.

"My pet pig," Granny said impatiently, as if anyone, even a newcomer, should know who Albert was. "Althea's got that pig all fat, and she can make a bunch of money selling him for bacon at the Charleston Flea Market."

Maggie took a deep breath. This was going to be a long story.

"Go on, Granny," Jim said. "What's your point?"

"Nothin' wrong with Albert eatin' my dog Jake's food. Althea claimed it was bad for him. She gave me a bunch of money and took

78

Albert to live with her and the pig she already had. Tol' me I could visit ever' day if I wanted to. Now that no-good woman was tryin' to marry Cotton, bless his soul. She come to my house about a month ago. Wanted me to put a spell on Cotton's wife. Said Delores was tryin' to take all his money. She wanted him for her own self."

"And did you put a spell on Delores?" Bill asked.

"Is it against the law?" Granny answered cautiously.

"Don't think so," he replied, trying to stifle a grin.

"Well, anyhow, Delores told Cotton she wanted a divorce, and Althea was happy. Then she goes and does this."

"Does what?" Maggie asked wearily.

"Gets Albert fat to sell him. If she was gonna marry Cotton, why did she need the money? Besides, she gave me a bunch of money to take Albert to her place. I bought the old fridge from the Tabby Café when she gave me all that cash. The one I had didn't defrost. This one does. I cain't give the money back, but, Maggie, you got to talk to her. I cain't buy poor baby Albert back, but if she sells him for bacon, I'm not never gonna to see him ag'in."

Maggie couldn't decide if she wanted to laugh or cry. "Maybe Althea will let me buy him back for you."

"That woman don't deserve one red cent," Granny shouted. "You go over there tomorrow—or better yet, tonight while it's dark—and take him."

Bill cleared his throat. "You want Maggie to steal him?"

Granny glared at the lawman in a fury. "I'll put a hex on you if you try to stop us," she declared menacingly. Then she added, in a placating manner, "You know, Bill, Althea was mistreatin' that pig, and you can report her to the animal shelter."

Maggie stood up. "It's after midnight. It's too late for any of us to be running around the island," she said firmly. "I'm going to bed. Hannah, will you lock up for me? Good night, everyone."

Jim kissed Maggie on one cheek, and Paul kissed the other. She left them standing at the door. Granny slipped out the back door, but not before she winked at Hannah and remarked, "Maggie'll help me. She ain't let me down yet."

Maggie heard Hannah turn the deadbolt and walk upstairs.

Maggie eased her sore muscles into bed and snapped off the lamp. But she couldn't go to sleep. Her mind was swirling with the events of the last few days. Maybe she should have given Cotton's money to Bill instead of hiding it in the attic. Then Althea might never get her hands on it. If only Maggie knew if the money was connected to Cotton's death or if he was only trying to hide it from his estranged wife. She finally drifted off to sleep, and when she opened her eyes, she was surprised to see the sun shining brightly through the window. Her clock said it was 7:22 A.M., the perfect time to get over to Althea's. Maybe she could catch Althea at home this early in the morning. Maggie left a note for Hannah and dropped Kibbles into Possum's bowl on her way out.

The air was cool, and Maggie strolled to Althea's bungalow without breaking a sweat. She found Althea in her back yard, squatting over a box full of squealing piglets.

"Come looka here," Althea called. "Granny's gonna be so pleased. Albert had babies." Althea giggled. "I guess we better change his name to Alberta. My pig Clyde figured out Albert was a sow. She kept getting fatter and fatter, and I couldn't figure out why. Ain't Granny gonna be pleased? She can raise these little ones."

Maggie laughed so hard, she almost fell over.

Ten or twelve piglets—some of them all pink and some of them spotted brown—squealed and clambered over each other inside the box. None of Maggie's Rosemont friends would believe a story like this. How could Granny not know her pig was female? Well,

80

Granny always was a bit loony, and her eyesight wasn't what it used to be.

"You should go get Granny and bring her down here to see the pigs," Maggie said. "She'll know the right name for Albert. I like 'Empress of Seaward' myself."

Althea squinted up at Maggie, looking doubtful. Obviously, she had never read any P.G. Wodehouse.

Althea scratched a pink little snout. "I might let 'em sleep at Granny's sometime—as long as she don't feed 'em dog food."

"Granny's really worried about Albert," Maggie said. "Go on over and explain it to her this morning. She was afraid you'd sell Albert for bacon."

Maggie paused, wondering how Althea would take her next question.

"Listen, I've been meaning to ask you about your relationship with Cotton. See, I've had some weird things happen to me since his death, and I thought you could help me figure out what's going on."

Althea looked like she might cry. "I loved Cotton. We was plannin' to settle here on Seaward. He was gonna build onto my place. Then he got a offer for a big job. I think it was in Savannah. He wanted me to leave my animals and go over there with him. I just didn't know what to do." Althea's lower lip trembled. "Wish I'd said I'd go. He might be alive now."

"Did he tell you who wanted to hire him in Savannah? Did they give him money to start the job? None of this is making sense."

"Once I told him I didn't want to go to Savannah to live, he started actin' pretty glum, and he didn't come 'round for a while. Then he got loose from Delores for good and he come back. I just wish we'd moved to Savannah." A tear trickled down Althea's cheek.

81

Maggie bent to give her a hug. "Don't worry. Bill will find Cotton's killer. If you remember anything else, let me know, okay?"

Maggie turned to go, but then she remembered something else. "By the way, did Cotton know Salty George?"

"Everybody this side of Port Royal knows that man," Althea answered. "He paid Cotton last spring to fix the center console in that boat of his. All the wood rotted out. Cotton did a good job for him. Never did hear if Salty liked it."

Althea disappeared into her back door as Maggie walked around the house to the dirt road.

She was thinking over what Althea had told her; then she stopped short. Hadn't Salty George said he didn't know Cotton? She made up her mind to ask him about it. By now, it seemed to Maggie that everybody on the island was a suspect. Everyone had hired Cotton or knew someone who had. Best to leave this for Bill, she reminded herself. But it didn't seem as if he was making any progress. He was always hanging around Hannah.

Maggie walked toward her cottage slowly, with her head down and her mind gnawing away at the mystery of Cotton's death. A shadow fell across the road in her path. She jumped, and then she heard Paul's voice.

"Good morning," he said. "Visiting with Althea? Hope she's still there. I've printed out diary entries from Sam Pepys."

Maggie looked at him blankly.

"You know, the Englishman, lived in the 1600s, kept a diary, wrote about the execution of King Charles the first?"

Maggie shook her head.

"Well, anyway, Althea seems to like this kind of stuff. There's an Internet site that publishes an entry from his diary every day. I made some copies for her." He leaned over and gave Maggie a peck on the cheek. "Hope to see you soon." As he walked away, he called back to her, "I hope you got all that pig business straightened out."

He added with a chuckle, "I think I'll eat turkey bacon for a while. I feel I almost know Albert personally now."

Maggie watched him walk away. *Strange*, she thought. *Why doesn't he just ask me out for a date?*

She considered going after him to ask that very question when she heard the boat horn from Salty George. She had sent a message telling him she wanted to talk to him about the Grady White. If Robert's mechanic had checked out the boat, she might be able to take it out today. She wondered if she should ask Salty George why he had denied knowing Cotton. Did it really matter? Maybe she had misunderstood him. Maybe the work Cotton had done for him just slipped his mind. Maggie hurried toward the dock where Salty George was headed. She got there just as he was tying the cleat. He shouted a greeting.

"Hey, Salty, do I get to use the Cash Floe?"

"Robert Davis' mechanic said you should take her out. She's in great shape. I've got an afternoon charter and thought I could give you a ride to the Beaufort marina. You can tie her up here and keep her for a few days. Want to do that?"

Maggie's eyes sparkled. "Do I ever!" She couldn't wait to get behind the wheel of a boat that might be hers soon. "Give me a minute to get my gear and see if Hannah wants to come."

She raced into the kitchen and skidded into Hannah's back. Hannah had been locked in an embrace with Bill. Maggie wondered about the forlorn look on Hannah's face, but she decided to mind her own business.

"I need to interview a few witnesses on the mainland, and the Mary Grace is due soon," Bill said. "You visit with Maggie. I'll come over tonight, and we'll go to the Seaward Plantation for dinner." He gave Hannah a kiss and was gone.

Hannah looked longingly out the door for a moment and then turned her gaze to Maggie. "What's your hurry?"

"We're going on a picnic on Sandibar Island. Salty will take us to pick up the boat. We can get food in Beaufort and give Possum a run on the beach." Hannah didn't look at all interested. "You can get some sun and be tan and beautiful for your date with Bill to-night." Maggie knew that would get Hannah moving. In a few minutes, their gear was stowed and they were skimming over the water. It was a perfect day for a picnic, sunny but not hot.

Maggie was so excited, she forgot to ask Salty George about Cotton.

Before long, she would wish she had.

Seven

Hannah tilted her face to the blue sky and closed her eyes. "I love the feel of the sun on my skin," she said. "This is the most fun I've had with you in ages. We worked too hard in Rosemont."

Maggie hadn't felt so relaxed in days, and she agreed wholeheartedly. "That's why I've simplified my life. I feel free when the ocean breeze is blowing through my hair, and I don't have to put anything on my face but sunscreen." She smiled affectionately at her friend. "I'm happy to have you here to enjoy it with me."

As always, Bill wasn't far from Hannah's thoughts. "It looks like Bill would stay if the sheriff retires," she said wistfully. "And if we get the Inn redo, I'll stay, too. I'd rather live in Beaufort, but I would come over to Seaward all the time. Guess our office would be your house."

The Cash Floe handled better than any boat Maggie had used for practice. "Thanks for putting the gas in for me," she said. "I got sandwiches and chicken from the general store. I'm glad you thought to grab extra water. Possum drinks a lot when we're out."

Possum heard her name and looked up eagerly. She was sprawled on the boat's deck with her paws wrapped around a red nylon traveling bowl.

Maggie steered the boat toward an island in the middle of Morgan Sound. When the tide was low, there was a full beach, a great place to look for shells. On the chart, the little island was labeled Sandibar. Maggie thought of it as paradise. She never saw anybody else around when she and Robert came there last summer. The isle faced the Intracoastal Waterway, but the sound of boat motors didn't drift that far.

"What are those silly white poles sticking out of the water?" Hannah asked.

Maggie glanced leeward. "Shrimp baiters," she said. "For about sixty days every year in the fall, the Department of Natural Resources opens the waters for taking shrimp with bait. Everybody in the lowcountry seems to have a different view on the subject. The license to bait costs twenty-five dollars, and I think there's a set limit. I don't think I'd want to do it. There are rules about the size of the pole you can use and the distance of the poles. Cotton told me the best time to bait shrimp is when the tide is starting to rise and—even better—when it's rising at dusk. Then, I think, the shrimp are in full migration." Maggie was suddenly sad. "Cotton knew a lot about the ways of the lowcountry. He was teaching me a lot. I miss him."

Hannah's ponytail, which she had pulled through the back of her Braves cap, whipped in the wind. "Would someone want to kill him if he knew they were going over their limit with the baiting?"

Maggie considered the question briefly and shook her head. "I can't imagine that anyone would fight over a few pounds of shrimp. I know the shrimpers are furious about foreign imports. A lot of the imported stuff doesn't taste as good as ours. We can throw my cast net and get our own off my dock. We don't need a permit for that." She stared out over the ocean, but she wasn't really concentrating on the view. "You know, you should probably share that theory of yours about the baiting limit with Bill. It might fit in with other information he has that we don't know about. Couldn't hurt, anyway. I have a gut feeling it was someone Cotton knew, even if it was just an employer from one of his jobs."

The women settled in for their ride. Maggie was confident of her abilities to handle the boat. She had been to Sandibar so many times with Robert that she knew where the sandbars were, and she had no problem reading the waters. She glanced at Hannah and knew by the dreamy smile on her face that she was thinking of Bill. The women were silent for a time, each lost in her own thoughts.

When Hannah finally spoke, she confirmed Maggie's suspicions about what she had been thinking. "Bill said he would call my cell phone this afternoon to let us know how the interview went with Delores. She's back in town, you know. Wants to claim the body and plan the service. Althea told Bill that was not what Cotton would want, though." Hannah reached into her pocket for her phone. "Oh, hell!" she exclaimed. "I must have left it on my bedside table. Oh, well, I'll call him when we get back."

Maggie felt a little uneasy when she realized that neither of them had a cell phone handy. But the boat radio must surely be in working order. After all, Robert would not send her out without reliable communication equipment. She hadn't asked Salty George about the radio at all, but even if he had given his okay, could she truly trust him? Well, there was no reason to mention the matter to Hannah. It would just upset her. And, anyway, it was such a beautiful day for a picnic. Maggie shook her head and banished any unpleasant thoughts. She had purchased some glorious food from a shop on Bay Street called Gourmet to Go, she was at the helm of this boat that might belong to her soon, and she and Hannah had landed a lucrative job at the Beaufort Inn. What more could she want?

"There's our island!" she called to Hannah. She maneuvered the boat toward the perfect spot to drop anchor.

Possum heard the excitement in Maggie's voice and responded by running wildly in circles. When the dog caught sight of gulls sunning themselves on the beach, she barked wildly. Possum loved to chase gulls.

It took almost twenty minutes to set anchor, unload the gear, and settle comfortably onshore. Maggie and Hannah shed their T-shirts, dropped sand chairs near the shoreline, and stretched out in their bikinis. Hannah rubbed lotion on her body, which already glowed with a golden tan.

"I'm amazed that you get so much sun in October, and it's still so warm," Hannah said. "This is a wonderful place."

Maggie lay back and closed her eyes. "I think this is my favorite time of the year in the lowcountry," she answered. "Summers are hot and humid, almost unbearably so sometimes, but fall is just right."

In just a few minutes, the women were ready to eat. Maggie threw Possum a soup bone. Possum snatched it up and wandered off down the beach. When the chicken sandwiches were gone, Maggie dramatically pulled out a package of brownies. "Ta-da!"

"My waistline is in terrible danger," Hannah groaned.

"Calories don't count when you're picnicking on Sandibar Island," Maggie said, handing a chocolate treat to her friend. "You don't get fat in paradise, no matter how much you eat."

Hannah nibbled at her brownie, but Maggie ate hers in three bites and licked her fingers.

Hannah closed her eyes and lay back, her face shaded by her cap, but she was smiling broadly. Her little green bikini clung to her curves.

"We did a great job with our presentation," Maggie said. "I hope nothing delays the project. I want to buy that boat."

"I hope Bill decides to stay here," Hannah replied. "He might decide to move back to Raleigh and finish his master's in psychology. He could be a profiler for any law enforcement agency in the country. I don't know if he really likes the lowcountry life. It frustrates him not to be able to track down his witnesses and talk to everybody in just a few days. I love it here, though. I could get used to this slow pace and all this quiet."

"Bill might not like the lowcountry, but he sure likes you," Maggie assured her friend. "Sheriff Hammond really wants to retire and move to Ocala. He has lots of family there. Bill might well decide he'd like to take the sheriff's place. If he finds Cotton's killer, he'd surely get elected. Is he making any headway?"

"He's waiting for the forensic report from the lab at the medical center in Charleston. He thinks we have too many suspects."

"I agree," Maggie answered. "Everybody knew Cotton, but not everybody would have a motive. His ex-wife looked good, but she was in New Mexico until yesterday, right?"

"Bill intends to check with the airlines. She could have come back sooner."

"What if she drove back or just pretended to leave?"

Hannah waved the question away. "Let's leave that kind of footwork to Bill and his deputies. He's got everyone on the force doing something to find the killer." Hannah's eyes popped open and she sat up. "Maggie, do you think we're safe? Someone tried to drown you, after all."

Maggie didn't want her friend to be frightened, so she answered carefully. "I think it was a joke that didn't seem so funny after I fell in. Sherm Pritchard is silly enough to do something like that to make a news story for his paper. I know that sounds far-fetched, but he's always desperate for real news, something that will boost circulation." Maggie screwed up her face in disgust. "You know, some people refer to reporters as vultures. But Sherm is more like a crab, scuttling around in the sand, hoping for someone to accidentally drop a tasty morsel."

Maggie chuckled, but Hannah frowned. "I'm going to share that theory with Bill," she said. "He's coming on the last run of the Mary Grace, and he'll be spending the night at the office in Markley Square."

"Maybe we should take the boat to Beaufort and give him a ride over. The Mary Grace could be so late that it skips our dock. I don't see how they're making any money. They aren't even staying on their regular route. I plan to have a word with Dianne. Robert is so disgusted, he's thinking of buying them out or starting his own ferry service. Anyway, if the killer came over on the Mary Grace, he was stuck on the island for a while—all night, probably. The first run that morning was late, as usual."

"What if the killer came over the night before and killed Cotton, then left the morning we found him?" Hannah speculated. "It would be easy to hide on Seaward and slip onto the ferry unde-tected. Why don't you ask Dianne who was on the boat that morn-ing when they left?" Hannah put her finger to her lips. "Let's not tell Bill this theory until you check it out, okay?"

"Fine with me," Maggie replied. "I think the killer wanted Cot-ton to be found sooner rather than later. The piling is around the center of activity at the marina. Does that mean his killer was a friend? Or the ex-wife? Somebody who felt at least some remorse?"

Hannah shuddered. "I keep thinking that we were shark bait with all that blood in the water."

"A shark attack that close to shore isn't likely," Maggie assured her friend. "The last one around here happened in 2001, I think, on Fripp Island. Happened to a tourist, a doctor, I believe. The shark took a chunk out of his leg. Now, in deep water…"

Hannah had heard enough. "Yuck. Let's not talk about this any-more. I want to enjoy this glorious day."

Possum romped up, demanding attention. Maggie stood, pro-duced a tennis ball from her bag, and threw it. Possum leaped after it, then brought it back, looking very pleased with herself. It was Possum's favorite game, and it went on until Maggie was bored to tears.

"At least we're getting some sun on the back of our legs," Maggie said. "Want to take a quick swim and wash the sand off? Then we'll pack up and go get Bill. Maybe he'll have that report, and he'll be able to narrow his list of suspects."

"Wish I could call him," Hannah grumped, "but I guess it'll be a nice surprise."

The sun was beginning to fade when Maggie and Hannah packed up their gear. It took a few minutes to convince Possum it was time to go. The tide had started to come in, and the water under the boat was much deeper than when they arrived. Maggie turned the Cash Floe's key, but nothing happened. She tried again, without success. The boat began to drift into the sound. "Maybe we should set the anchor again until I can get this Yamaha to turn over," she said.

"Let's just get this boat moving before dark," Hannah answered, sounding a little nervous.

It took a while for the women to wrestle the anchor into position in the rushing water. Maggie's arms hurt, and Hannah began to feel the evening chill. She grabbed a sweatshirt that had been thrown over a seat and slipped it on. Possum, on the other hand, wasn't suffering at all. She was snoozing on the deck after a long, exciting day.

Maggie turned the ignition key again. The engine coughed and died.

"Is it possible to flood this engine? Like a car?" she asked Hannah.

"I know nothing about cars and even less about boats. Has Salty George given you any lessons about being stranded?" Hannah looked perilously close to panic. Maggie knew she couldn't deal with hysterics right now, so she didn't tell Hannah the disturbing thought that had crossed her mind: If someone had tampered with the boat, might it blow up if she got it started?

"I'll call Robert on the boat radio," she said, trying to sound calm. "If he's not there, then someone else can tell us what to do. Just sit tight."

Maggie spoke into the radio's microphone, then released the transmit button and listened carefully. The only reply she heard was static. She switched channels and tried again. No one could hear her, apparently.

Hannah's eyes were wide with fear as darkness fell, and she hugged herself tightly in an effort to stop shaking. "Who checked out this boat? Salty George? I don't know if I trust him. I'm thinking sabotage." Hannah's voice got shriller with every word until she was wailing. "I might never see Bill again. We might never get a chance to show what we can do at the Ribaut Inn."

Maggie watched Hannah pace across the boat's aft while she continued to fiddle with the radio. She switched to channel twenty-two. She thought that might be the Coast Guard Station at Tybee. Then she tried sixty-eight. She thought for a second she heard a voice, but if that's what it was, it was drowned by static.

She remembered that Salty George had told her there were flares under the seat behind the captain's chair. She found the flares, but she couldn't find a flare gun. She stumbled as the boat shifted from side to side. She looked over the bow and realized the anchor wasn't holding.

"Quick, Hannah," she shouted, "we're drifting out to sea. Help me get this anchor set again. I can't see the island, and I don't know where we are. If we stay here for the night, we'll be able to chart a course tomorrow and maybe get the radio working. I have the boat's nightlights on. Maybe someone will see us."

They struggled with the anchor until the boat seemed to have stopped drifting, but it rocked violently in the waves.

"I think I'm going to be sick," Hannah whimpered.

"Not on the boat," Maggie yelled from her position at the radio. "Throw your head overboard."

"Do you want me to take it off my body?" Hannah began to laugh hysterically.

"Break, break," Maggie shouted into the radio. "This is Cash Floe. We are stranded somewhere near Sandibar Island. Anyone, please acknowledge." More static, then nothing. "I'm going to save the battery until morning," she told Hannah. "Let's settle in. There are blankets under the front seat. We can all snuggle together and have a little warmth."

Maggie and Hannah lay next to Possum, who was snoring softly. Possum woke long enough to lick Maggie's face.

There was no hope of sleep, so Maggie tried to remember everything she had learned about a boat's instruments. The GPS would give her a reading tomorrow, and in the daylight, she could avoid sandbars and at least go in the right direction—if she could get the boat started. It was the dark that frightened her, not the boat. She was still confident in her abilities as captain; she just couldn't figure out what was wrong with the boat.

"Are you awake?" Hannah whispered. "I keeping thinking, what if no one comes for us? What will we do?"

"We'll make paddles and row ourselves back," Maggie said confidently.

"But what if someone sabotaged us to strand us here? Wouldn't they come after us, maybe in the dead of night?"

"What do you suggest we do, Hannah?" Maggie snapped. "Shall we wait here patiently until someone comes to knife us? You can go first."

Hannah sobbed, causing Possum to jump in her sleep. "Stop it! Stop it! I'm scared!"

Maggie reached across Possum and took Hannah's hand. "I'm scared, too, but I'd rather not get myself all worked up with gruesome possibilities." She racked her brain for a more pleasant topic and finally seized on their business ventures. "You know, Ribaut Inn is very exciting, but we can't just depend on one job to get our company going. I'll ask Robert if he knows about any new condos on Hilton Head. I've been thinking that Chandler Morris doesn't have that laid-back lowcountry attitude. It'll be interesting working with him. He's not pompous or smug, though, and he's got a great business sense."

Hannah wasn't that easily distracted. "Unless he's a murderer," she declared. Maggie sighed, and Hannah instantly regretted her outburst. "I'm sorry, but I keep thinking that someone meant for us to be in this position."

Maggie forced herself not to lose patience. "Someone will realize in the morning that we never made it back home. Let's try to rest now." Possum's feet twitched, and Maggie chuckled. "Look, Possum is chasing rabbits in her sleep. Let's try to join her."

"I'd rather be chasing rainbows with Bill," Hannah mumbled.

Maggie listened to Hannah's breathing slow and knew she had drifted off to sleep. Maggie closed her eyes. It seemed like only a minute when she woke with a start and sat up. Possum was racing around the boat, looking for a patch of grass, apparently. "Wait, Possum, don't pee on the boat. I'll put you in the water."

The commotion roused Hannah. She stood up slowly and stretched her stiff muscles. Then she went completely still. "What's that noise?" she asked Maggie, who was struggling to pull the soaking dog back onboard. "Is that a boat motor?"

When Possum was safely on deck and had settled down again, Maggie could hear it, too. She turned her face to the sky. A helicopter flew into view, spinning the water into froth beneath it. Hannah and Maggie hugged each other and shrieked. Maggie dropped onto the deck, limp with relief. She wasn't sure if the sounds coming from Hannah meant she was laughing or crying.

"We're in the Beaufort River," she told Hannah, "near the Marine Corps Air Station."

Maggie recognized the helicopter circling above them as an Angel One. She and Hannah grabbed towels, clothing, whatever they could lay their hands on, and waved frantically.

94

The two women were so occupied with the helicopter, they didn't notice that a boat had pulled up beside them. The noise from the helicopter had drowned out the sound of its engine.

Maggie wasn't sure what made her look around, but when she did, she spotted a man she had never seen before, and he was trying to board her boat. She glanced up at the helicopter for help, but how would the pilot know that they were about to be kidnapped? He might think the stranger was trying to help them. The stranger planted one foot on the deck, and Maggie knew she had to act. She ran across the deck and shoved the stranger with all her might. He fell backwards, but as Maggie leaned over and scanned the water, she saw the man surface almost immediately.

Then she heard a familiar voice. It was Robert, and he was laughing.

She looked around in surprise. Three boats had pulled beside the Cash Floe. Robert stood on the deck of the one closest, surrounded by men and women in some type of uniform. "You just knocked Dennis Collins overboard. He's the skipper of the Beaufort Water Search and Rescue team," he shouted, and he started laughing again.

Eight

Maggie and Hannah clambered onto the rescue boat. Maggie averted her eyes as she passed by the dripping skipper.

Dennis and some of his crew boarded the Cash Floe to examine her engine.

"I can't figure it out," Robert told Maggie. "My mechanic checked that boat carefully."

He had brought with him a thermos of coffee, some sweet rolls, and fresh fruit from the restaurant. He poured the ladies a cup of steaming java and let them savor the coffee in peace for a few minutes before handing them each a sweet roll. This time, Hannah didn't complain about her waistline. She devoured the roll and reached for another.

"We heard your calls for help," Robert said when the ladies had filled their stomachs. "But you couldn't hear us. I finally figured you didn't know how to adjust the squelch on the radio. I knew the radio had to be fine, but I can't figure out what could have gone wrong with the motor. Maybe you got some bad fuel."

"She's got no fuel at all," Dennis interrupted. "The tank is empty. When did you last fill 'er up?"

Maggie whirled to face Hannah. "Didn't you put fuel in yesterday while we were at the marina?"

Hannah's face turned crimson. "We didn't need any," she protested. "I tried putting it in that hole," she added, pointing to the fishing rod holder, which was on the opposite side of the boat from the gas tank. "The gas just ran right back out, so I thought it was full."

The skipper, already not particularly enchanted with these two women, looked downright furious. He put his hands on his hips and glared at Robert. "Okay, we'll tow her back, but teach these women how to fill up a gas tank before their next trip."

Now Maggie's face was red. She pointed sternly at Robert. "Don't you tell a soul about this."

"Please don't tell Bill I did that," Hannah pleaded, nearly in tears. "He'll think I'm an idiot."

Robert grinned. "I'm making no promises. A story this good can't be kept under wraps. The rescue crew will tell, even if I don't."

The skipper was in a foul mood all the way back to Palmetto Bluff Marina. But then Robert pulled out a wad of bills and slapped them into Dennis' hand. "This is my donation to Beaufort's volunteer rescue team," Robert announced grandly. For the first time since Maggie laid eyes on him, Dennis smiled. Maggie fervently hoped she'd never have to see his face again, and she was sure he felt the same way about her.

Robert loaned the ladies his golf cart, and he walked back to the Tabby Café, where Jim was planning his menu for the weekend.

Possum seemed as happy as Hannah and Maggie to be home. The dog headed for the back yard, and the women headed straight for the shower. Then they met back in the kitchen for a cup of coffee and a review of yesterday's events.

"At least no one was trying to sabotage us," Maggie said, trying to find a silver lining in their cloud of mistakes and embarrassments. "When are you going to call Bill?"

"I tried the minute we got here. He was out of the office on the mainland trying to track down a witness. He'll call when he gets my message. I just wanted to let him know we're home safe."

Maggie glanced at the *Seaward Times*, which she had brought in from the paper box. The top headline on the front page caught her attention. Sherman had written an article about Chandler Morris, which said he was to be Seaward's newest resident. The article implied that he was buying the Myers place next door to Robert and that developing the island might be in his plans. Sherman wrote that there was a possibility that Chandler's plans included a second gated community with an initial spec house to show interested buyers. Maggie snatched up the phone to call Robert. He used to be a builder and had worked with Chandler on a project in Charleston.

Jim Hamilton answered the phone on the third ring. "Sorry, Maggie," he said. "Robert went to his house for a nap. Seems he was up all night looking for you and Hannah." Maggie heard a muffled chuckle on the other end of the line. "Why don't you come over for dinner? We're doing my special this evening, the seafood trough. I think Hannah and Bill would enjoy a real lowcountry boil."

"Count us in," Maggie said. "My mouth is already watering. We'll see you at six." Maggie hung up the phone and filled Hannah in on the plans she'd made.

"What's a seafood trough? Sounds like something you'd feed sea horses." Hannah giggled at her own joke.

"You won't be laughing when you taste it," Maggie insisted. "Jim and Robert built these small troughs that go in the middle of the table. They pour in the seafood boils, and everybody helps themselves."

"What kind of seafood is it?"

"It's not just seafood. Shrimp goes in, but so do Polish sausage, ears of corn, lemon, garlic, Worcestershire, maybe just a tablespoon, and then Jim pours in his secret seasoning. I'm not sure Robert even knows what that seasoning is. It boils all together, but not for too long. And then we pig out!" Maggie snapped her fingers. "That reminds me. I guess I'd better find out if Granny and Althea got their pig issue settled. I think I'll walk over that way. I need some exercise anyway."

Hannah yawned. "I'm going to take a nap and then try to call Bill again. By the way, what does one wear to belly up to a trough?"

Maggie ignored the question and walked away with a wave. The chilly morning had given way to a glorious afternoon. Maggie noticed the marsh had changed almost overnight from green to golden brown. As she passed by the Red Eye, she heard loud voices. It didn't sound like anyone she knew. She knew she should just walk on by, but she was curious. She slipped around the corner and looked in the back door. A man with a Spanish accent was saying something Maggie couldn't understand. A much louder voice, also with an accent, answered.

Dickie walked in from the main dining room and saw Maggie through the screen door.

"Come on in," he called. "I heard you spent the night on the river. You okay?"

Maggie grimaced. "Word travels fast around here. I was on my way to Granny's, and I heard a bit of a commotion. New employees?"

"I hired a couple guys from Oxicana, Mexico. They were here to do the tomato crop, and since they had green cards, they wanted to stay. They're teaching Little Lavender to cook some spicy stuff he never tried before. Burnt my mouth out last night. Sallie Jo won't even touch it. She did say she's prob'ly goin' back to the mainland to have my boy, though. Thanks for talkin' to her." Dickie swung open the screen door. "Wanna come in and try the tacos they're stirring up?"

Maggie shook her head. "I'm trying to sort out the pig problem between Althea and Granny. Then Hannah and I are having dinner at the Tabby tonight. Jim is planning a lowcountry boil. Hannah and Bill have never had that."

Dickie scowled. "Does Robert know that Jim tried to hire Lav right out from under me? Told Lav him and Cotton were gonna build a restaurant in Savannah." Dickie clenched his fists. "That

99

man better watch it. I don't care for somebody tryin' to steal my chef, 'specially since I'm payin' for his cooking classes at Tech."

"I heard about all that months ago, but things have changed since then," Maggie assured Dickie. "I think Jim is planning to stay with Robert. I'll ask him tonight, just to set your mind at ease, but I know Lavender won't leave you. Anyway, Jim doesn't have Cotton as a partner anymore, does he?"

Dickie didn't lose his scowl.

"Don't you think you're being a bit unreasonable, my friend?" Maggie asked gently. "I mean, it's pretty normal for chefs to move around, isn't it?"

"It's pretty normal for restaurants to go under, too, but it sure as hell ain't happening to mine," Dickie growled. Then he gave Maggie an apologetic smile. "Tell Granny no matter how hard up we get, I won't let Lav fry up Albert. I heard she was worried we was plannin' to buy Albert and roast him."

Maggie could still hear Dickie laughing as she walked down the road toward Granny's house. She hadn't gotten far when Paul called to her from his house on the hill. He trotted down to meet her. "We've got to quit meeting like this," he said with a wink. "I was just about to go for a stroll. I've got a bad case of writer's block, and I thought a little fresh air might help. I've got my hero into a mess, and I can't seem to get him out. So what have you been up to?"

"You must be the only one in Seaward who hasn't heard about our rescue."

Paul took off his sweater and placed it gallantly on the grass next to the road. He motioned for Maggie to have a seat. "Tell me," he said.

The more Maggie talked, the harder Paul laughed. She was offended at first, and then she began to laugh, too. They were laughing so hard, neither one of them heard Jim walk through the grass behind them.

"I was on my way back from the Tabby, and I heard all this cackling and carrying on," Jim said. "Sounded like a bunch of seagulls shrieking. If you aren't too tired, Maggie, let's go ahead and plan that wine-tasting for Robert. That way, I'll be able to start ordering tomorrow."

Maggie stood up, brushed off her slacks, and handed Paul his sweater. "Sounds great to me. Want to help, Paul?"

"I have to figure out how to save my hero in the next few pages. I better get back to my PC. What's for dinner tonight, Jim? Even a blocked writer has to eat."

Jim smiled, but he didn't look particularly happy. "My special seafood trough. You won't want to miss that."

When Paul had disappeared into his house, Jim pulled out a notebook and pen and looked at Maggie expectantly. This was not like the high-powered planning sessions she had done with her Rosemont associates. But it was good enough, she figured, and where else could she plan a wine-tasting sitting on the grass in the fall sunshine? She plopped back down, and Jim sat beside her, still waiting.

"Let's include an oyster roast down by the dock," she began. "That gives us room for more people. Robert has thirty or more reservations, and we just started inviting people. Oh, and add some of the new types of beer from breweries in the area."

Jim looked doubtful. "That's not the type of party I had in mind. We can have people inside the Tabby and require coat and tie. We can charge more."

Maggie shook her head. "Jim, how many tourists do you know who keep a coat and tie on their sailboats? Some do, but we'll have more fun and more participants if we go casual. Why not make sauces for the oysters? Maybe even bottle some for the guests to take with them. Have the Tabby Café logo on the bottles."

Jim looked more glum than ever. "What kind of sauces are you talking about?"

"Haven't you ever been to an oyster roast? I thought you were from the lowcountry."

Jim grunted in disgust. "Never could stand the sight of the slimy little blobs."

Maggie shrugged. "You're the chef. Experiment. I like a catsup-based cocktail sauce myself. Or even a remoulade."

"Creative I can be," Jim responded. "There's a new microbrewery in Charleston making a brew called Palmetto something. Ale maybe. I'll try to get them to come promote their product—with free samples, of course."

Maggie rewarded him with a grateful smile and a slap on the back. "Now you're getting into the spirit of the thing! Inside the Tabby, we can have wine, cheese, and crackers. Robert may have authentic oyster tables in his garage. Let's go ask him. He's always at the dock in late afternoon, isn't he? I also want to know if I can take the boat out again." Jim raised his eyebrows, but Maggie kept talking. "I'm determined to buy the Cash Floe and be independent on the water."

Jim followed Maggie as she strode toward the restaurant.

"I had an elaborate meal planned for the wine-tasting, but I understand your point of view," Jim said. "If Robert wants it casual, then we can go with it. We could just have finger sandwiches, veggie trays, but not the sit-down meal. It'll be about the wine and not the food."

Maggie nodded her approval. "My grandmother always told me it was okay to serve ice cream in your champagne glasses as long as you had the sorbet crystal in the china cabinet where guests could see it. Everyone knows you are a great chef, Jim. They don't know

102

that you can do more than sit-down meals. Let's show them." Maggie looked back at Jim to see if had understood. He looked like he was mulling it over, at least, but he kept quiet.

They found Robert staring at the Cash Floe. He greeted Maggie with a sympathetic grin. "Feeling better?" he asked. "I want you to get back on this boat real soon. We'll just always make sure you have gas and a gun for your flares." His mouth twitched with suppressed laughter. "Planned that party?" he asked Jim.

Maggie explained her ideas, with Jim occasionally chiming in. Robert nodded enthusiastically while they talked. "It's still early for the best oysters, but let's give it a shot," he said. "I'll get the tables. Dickie already told me he was closing that night. He's going to lend us his crew. We'll put Lav on roasting. He's the best in the lowcountry—still uses burlap bags to steam the little critters. Everybody from Annapolis to the Keys will be talking about our party at the Tabby Café."

Maggie suddenly remembered that she still hadn't talked to Granny. She had to hurry because she'd have to go home and change for dinner. She explained hastily to Robert, and she and Jim walked back toward the road. "Hannah and I are still waiting on a call from Chandler Morris so we can get started decorating the cottages at the Ribaut Inn," she remarked.

"Chandler Morris? The builder?"

"Yes, you know him, don't you, Jim?" She looked up at Jim just as he pushed a dark curl away from his forehead. He looked so handsome, her breath caught in her throat. His piercing eyes made her feel that he could read her thoughts, and she blushed. They stared silently at each other for a long moment.

"Are you being careful?" Jim asked. Maggie was surprised. It was not what she had expected him to say. If he saw her disappointment, he gave no sign. "Robert says they haven't a clue as to who pushed you in the water," he continued. "And are you sure that boat just needed gas and nothing else was wrong with it?"

"If someone wanted to kill me, why didn't they knock me in the head before they shoved me in the river?" she said, trying to keep her voice light.

When they reached the door to the Tabby, Maggie turned to Jim to say her goodbyes. He leaned over and brought his lips down to hers, but she pulled away. "Well," she stammered, "I guess I'll get going." She couldn't look into Jim's face. She was too embarrassed. She had no idea how he had reacted to her rejection.

But when he spoke, he sounded calm and friendly. "I'll call when I have the list Robert wants. See you tonight."

Maggie rushed away without looking back, mentally kicking herself every step of the way. Jim was such a good-looking guy, and he seemed perfectly nice. Why hadn't she just let him kiss her? Something inside her just wasn't ready for that first kiss and what it might lead to.

Maggie realized she was almost running down the road, but she didn't slow her pace. In just moments, she was trotting into Granny's yard. Sallie Jo waddled out of the house to meet her, holding her enormous belly with one hand and adjusting a pink curler in her hair with the other. "If you've come to see Granny, she's gone to Althea's," she said. "She's goin' to make sure that sow of hers has enough food. Granny says they ain't sellin' any of Alberta's offspring. We may all get pet pigs for Christmas."

Maggie's eyes widened in horror. "Possum wouldn't like sharing her doggie treats with a pig. I hope you're joking."

Sallie Jo gave Maggie a look of resigned exasperation. "I wish I was. Granny's crazy, you know." She emphasized her point with a nod, which set her curlers bouncing. "She has it in her head that this big, white bird swooped down and is goin' to kill everybody in their sleep at night and then head south—or some such thing. Where does she get this nonsense?"

Maggie laughed. "She's talking about the snowbirds—the tourists—coming here for the winter. These people escape the snow up North and follow the sunshine to the South."

Sallie Jo shook her head, and the curlers did another dance. "Now, why would anybody want to leave their home? I'm only gonna stay on the mainland as long as I got to. The doctor told me yesterday if this baby is healthy, I can leave the hospital and come right home the next day."

"If I have my boat by then, I'll come to the mainland and bring you home."

"Now, ain't that nice of you. You're gonna be my baby's godmother. As soon as we pick out a name, I'll let you know. But, Maggie? About that ride from the mainland after the baby's born?" Sallie brought a thumb to her mouth and chewed her nail.

"Yes?" Maggie prodded.

"Well, you'll make sure you got plenty of gas, right? I don't mean to offend. It's just that, with a new baby and all..." Sallie's head shook violently as she struggled to express herself without giving offense, and one curler escaped her tightly coiled hair, fell at her feet, and rolled off the porch.

Maggie had to laugh. "I promise," she said.

Sallie Jo decided it was time to change the subject. "That new sheriff might just as well look in the Everglades for Cotton's killer, for all the good his investigation is doin'. Everybody around these parts liked Cotton a lot. Didn't you?"

"I'll never find another carpenter like him, but he was my friend, too," Maggie said softly. "He knew me so well, he knew how to build what I wanted before I could tell him. We will all miss him."

"Even his ex-wife, Delores, musta cared about him. She gave him a good deal, it turns out."

105

"What kind of a deal?" Maggie asked.

"The judge, he done told them to split everything all down the middle. They didn't have much to split. But they couldn't split that singlewide in half, now could they? So they sold it, but Delores was so excited about getting' on to New Mexico—Taos, I think it was—she told Cotton he could have whatever he could get for the trailer. I heard he got something like fifteen thousand." Sallie looked at Maggie with wide eyes. "It was in good condition, but fifteen thousand? Lawdy, lawdy."

Maggie opened her mouth, closed it, and finally managed to speak without letting Sallie Jo know how upset she was. "How on earth do you know this?"

"Mama's sister, Aunt Marty. She lives in the same trailer park on the other side of Ridgeland. She knows the man what paid the money for it. Cotton moved in with Althea, and the man rented it out."

Maggie realized that the money Cotton left for her was from the sale of his trailer. He had trusted her, obviously. But what was she supposed to do with it?

Nine

Hannah slathered sunscreen on her arms and flipped onto her stomach in a lounger on Maggie's deck. "I had a great time last night," she said. "That lowcountry boil is a great dish. And, as my dad used to say, Jim Hamilton thinks you're quite a dish, too."

Maggie didn't respond. Her mind was on the hidden money. She knew she had to tell Bill soon—unless it had nothing to do with Cotton's death. If it was his share of the divorce money, would he want it to go to Althea? Was he killed for the money? She wished she could talk to Cotton and ask him these questions. Could Cotton have been out in the middle of the night bringing her the money? Or did he come over on the last run of the Mary Grace? Maggie heard Hannah call her name, sounding exasperated.

"Sorry," Maggie said. "My mind is wandering today. Maybe we'll hear from Chandler. If not, we need to finish pulling the samples for Caroline and send them to Rosemont. Glad she still wants to consult with me. She's not going to be happy if you decide to stay here."

"I'll fax a copy of what we've decided," Hannah said. "If she wants more, we can do that later. The mosquito magnets you bought really work." She held out an arm. "See? No ugly red bumps. I love not working on a tranquil October day. And being on a barrier island off the coast of South Carolina. It's more like an exotic retreat on the other side of the world."

Maggie had been trying to concentrate on what Hannah was saying, and she nodded absently. "Seaward Island is a different approach to living. Centuries away from Rosemont and the everyday lifestyle of our upstate friends. That reminds me. I haven't talked to

Althea or Granny. I think they have the pig issue settled, but I better check. I'll try Althea's place this morning."

Maggie left Hannah to sizzle in the noonday sun. It felt like mid-June, warm and breezy. As she walked toward the road, she thought about the boat. She couldn't buy it until Chandler gave the final go-ahead. Then she could justify a boat for trips to the mainland whenever she needed to check on the project at the Ribaut Inn.

She was deep in thought and didn't see Paul step in her path until she banged her head into his shoulder. "Watch where you're stepping," he said with a laugh. She looked up in surprise, and he gave her a smile and a wink.

"Could I interest you in reading an entry in Sam Pepys' diary?" he asked. "Thought I might get you hooked on this Internet site. I just stepped out for a respite. I started working last night and didn't get away for the lowcountry boil. Have a good time?" He matched his stride to Maggie's as she headed toward Althea's place. Maggie noticed that his muscles strained against the ACE Basin T-shirt he was wearing. *Looks good*, she thought.

The pair walked up the front steps together, and Maggie looked through the screen into the tiny living room. It was as cluttered as before. The air conditioner was on, and cool air rushed out through the screen. Maggie thought of her brother, Bill, standing in front of the fridge with the door open, cooling off the kitchen. Their mother would always yell when she caught him doing that.

Maggie called to Althea through the screen door, but no one answered.

"Let's walk around the house," Maggie said. "Maybe she's feeding the animals."

The noises in the back yard—squeals and grunts and growls—reminded Maggie of the Atlanta zoo. She caught a glimpse of someone moving through the trees that surrounded Althea's property. Whoever it was wore a black T-shirt. The shadowy figure disappeared into the woods so quickly, Maggie wondered if she was seeing things.

Maggie scanned the yard and saw Althea lying by the pigsty just outside the tree line. She yelled Althea's name and ran to help her. Paul followed at her heels.

Maggie felt for a pulse. Althea groaned and opened her eyes. "What happened?" Maggie demanded. "Are you all right?"

"I was looking at the piglets and felt a pain in the back of my head," Althea said weakly. She tried to get up but slumped back to the ground, moaning.

"Granny wouldn't do something like this to get even, would she?" Paul asked. "Here's my cell phone. You call 9-1-1 while I get her in the house. How long will it take an ambulance to get here?"

Maggie snorted in disgust. "At least a couple of days," she said. "If we could find the Mary Grace and get the car tow to load the ambulance. We can call Walt Casey. He's a great vet."

Paul looked at Maggie with alarm. "Did you say vet? I'm never getting sick over here."

Althea sat up slowly and gingerly touched her head. "Don't need Walt," she said. "Big knot back there. My noggin's gonna ache for a week."

"What happened?" Maggie asked. "Did you see anyone?"

Althea shook her head, then instantly regretted it. "Ow! That hurts," she complained. "I was feeding the pigs and thinking about Sadie. Almost time for her to have her puppies. I hope she didn't run off. Keep an eye out for her. Anyhow, as I leaned over the pen, I thought I felt a breeze on my neck and then boom! Next thing I knew, y'all were standing over me. Help me up. I want to go inside."

With Paul supporting her on one side and Maggie on the other, Althea walked shakily up her back steps and into her tiny kitchen.

Paul glanced at his watch. "It's later than I thought. I have a conference with my agent. Call if you need me."

Maggie watched, annoyed, as he left. "Just like that, he leaves," she said. "Now what am I supposed to do?"

"Make tea," Althea answered. "Suppose someone was looking for Cotton? I know Granny wouldn't get mad enough to whack me. She's happy about Albert—um, Alberta."

Maggie put the kettle on to boil, and with Althea's guidance, got a lemon from a bowl on the table and sugar from the cupboard. The Earl Grey tea bags steeped in a pot with the same Blue Willow pattern Maggie's mother had used for everyday service. She poured Althea a strong, hot cup and instructed her to sip it slowly.

"I guess somebody's after me for the money Cotton left me," Althea commented between sips. "He told me not to tell. But maybe word got out. He gave me fifteen thousand to start my flea market finds shop. Already put a deposit on the building down in Port Royal. The money is in the bank. I wadn't about to leave it layin' around the house."

Maggie stared at Althea in amazement. The money Cotton left at her house must not have been for Althea. What was it for, then?

"Did Cotton give you all his money? Did he tell you where he got it?"

"From his divorce," Althea answered. "From Delores. She left and told him she never wanted to see this dump again. How could she not love this part of the world? Always complainin' about heat, humidity, and bugs. Never satisfied." Althea waved a hand in dismissal. "Good riddance, I say."

"Did Cotton say anything about giving money to someone else?" Maggie persisted. "To keep for him or anything?"

"I thought he gave it all to me. Can you help me up? I'm goin' over to Granny's, get her to hex whoever did this to me. Maybe get a poultice for the back of my head. Maybe I'll stay over there tonight. Whoever conked me might just come back."

"Good idea," Maggie responded. "I'll get Bill Johnson over here to check everything out. We'll put the word out that the money's in the bank. If that is what the person was looking for, you'll be safe. Did Cotton tell you anything that might be important? Try to remember." Althea shook her head. "Well, if you think of anything, let me know."

"You think maybe Delores changed her mind and sent someone to hurt me and take the money?"

Maggie sighed. "Anything is possible, but I doubt it. Are we having a service for Cotton on the island?"

"Naw," Althea answered. "I sent him back to Edgefield. He's got family there, sisters and all." Althea wiped away a tear. "I'll always remember him."

Althea was still wobbly when she locked the doors and walked across her yard, so Maggie clutched her arm.

"Granny'll feed the animals and get Sadie for me," Althea said.

"I'll help, too," Maggie said. "Just let me know what I can do."

Maggie walked Althea to the fence at Granny's and left the two women talking.

She took the long way home to Lawson's Creek. She wanted time to think. The same thought kept echoing through her mind. Someone who lived on Seaward or was familiar with the area, at least, had killed Cotton. Either for money or information. It looked like nobody was safe until this person was caught. But the people she knew on Seaward were not killers.

When Maggie walked into her yard, she found Hannah asleep in a hammock in the shade of a live oak. Possum met Maggie at the door, wagging her tail enthusiastically. Before Maggie could greet the dog properly, the phone rang, and Possum whimpered with disappointment when she didn't get the attention she thought she deserved. Maggie picked up the telephone on the second ring.

She was surprised to hear Chandler Morris' voice.

"Maggie," he began, "I want you to meet my sister Marianna. Will you and Ms. Graham come into Beaufort sometime tomorrow? We have a few questions for you two."

"Of course. What time's good for you?"

"Any time after four. I've got to be on Hilton Head for a lunch meeting. Will you be around your house this afternoon? There's a fellow who wants to come see you. I'm sending him over on the ferry. Juan's my best carpenter, and he'll do a great job on that porch you were telling us about. See you tomorrow."

Chandler disconnected before Maggie could say another word.

As Maggie set down the receiver, Hannah walked in and gave her a lazy smile. "Did you get the pig fight settled?"

Maggie took a deep breath. "So much has happened, I forgot that's why I went out there to Althea's in the first place."

While Maggie filled Hannah in, Possum raced around the kitchen, growling. "Settle down, girl," Maggie scolded. "That's no way to play in the house." She shooed Possum out the doggie door.

Hannah was more interested in Bill's impending arrival than anything Maggie had to say. "I've got to get ready," she said and headed upstairs to the shower. "Chandler wouldn't ask us to come into town unless he wanted to give us the go-ahead in person," she called over her shoulder as she bounded up the stairs.

Just as Hannah slammed her bedroom door, Maggie heard ferocious growls and shouts of panic coming from the back yard. She raced outside to find that Possum had cornered a rumpled boy, who looked to be in his teens, wearing patched jeans and scuffed sandals. Maggie pulled Possum away from the boy with another scolding, and the Lab slunk away, but not before she gave the boy a final warning growl.

"Juan is here to make your porch look pretty," the boy announced. "Mr. Chandler Morris say to tell you I stay until it is finished. He say you will give me a good lunch and let me work at my own pace. This is so?"

"This is so," she answered. What else could she say if she was going to work for Chandler? He was trying to do her a favor, and she certainly wasn't going to insult him by turning the boy away. "When will you start?"

"At this moment. Show me the porch and the tools."

Maggie led Juan through the front of the cottage out to the sleeping porch. Beside the house in a neat pile were the tools and materials that Maggie had purchased. She explained what she wanted to the young carpenter and then looked at him closely to see if he understood. "Any questions?" she asked. "Have you had lunch today?"

"I do not eat before the boat comes to bring me here," Juan answered. He peered at Maggie curiously. "Why do you want a porch to sleep on when you have beautiful house and nice bed?"

Maggie laughed. "It's hard to explain. I'll give you something to eat now. We'll call it tea time."

Juan followed Maggie back to the kitchen. He laughed with delight when he saw Possum slide through her doggie door. Maggie began to pile leftovers onto the French pine farm table that served as her dining table and kitchen island. She remembered wonderful meals on this table in Rosemont. She had found it in an antique shop on a buying trip for the design firm. Juan pulled out a chair and seemed to enjoy every bite of shrimp salad and thick bakery bread, served with creamy butter and slabs of thick, ripe tomatoes. Robert grew them and other veggies in his greenhouse and supplied Maggie all year.

Hannah wandered in, dressed for her date with Bill, and helped herself to some shrimp salad. While she ate, Maggie explained that Juan would be building the sleeping porch. Juan stood to put his plate in the sink just as Possum started barking frantically again. Maggie opened the back door. Robert, accompanied by a woman about his age, stepped into the room.

The woman was not conventionally pretty, but she was striking. Her jaw was square, and her cheekbones prominent. Her thick dark hair, streaked with auburn highlights, was pulled back into a neat bun. She was dressed in designer jeans and a cashmere twin set that showed off a girlishly slim figure.

"I want you to meet Marianna, Chandler Morris' sister," Robert said. "She's over here looking at the house that's for sale next to mine, the Myers house. Too bad they moved, but lucky for me to have such a lovely lady moving in next door."

Marianna accepted the compliment without any signs of embarrassment. "The house is beautiful, and I need a designer who can understand what I want and not what they want to sell me," she told Maggie as the two women shook hands.

"So you're definitely going to buy it?" Maggie asked.

"I've already made an offer. I'll know shortly whether they will accept."

"So it was you and not Chandler with plans to buy the house," Maggie remarked. "Doesn't Sherm ever get anything straight? He wrote that Chandler had his eye on the house with plans for development out here."

"I'm tired of living in town. I want some peace and quiet," Marianna said.

Maggie motioned for Robert and Marianna to sit down at the table. She set to work making coffee.

The three of them made small talk about the island for a few minutes, and then Hannah interrupted. "So you want to hire Lowcountry Interiors to decorate your house?" she asked eagerly.

The women began to discuss the house and Marianna's ideas for decorating it. Maggie and Hannah kept exchanging excited glances.

They both knew that, with this job and Chandler's, their firm was off to a very good start.

Marianna reached into her elegant Gucci purse and pulled out her checkbook. She signed a check with a flourish and handed it to Maggie. "Here's a deposit," she said. "If my offer to buy is accepted, I'll get you a key. I hope to be in the house by Christmas."

She stood, and Robert followed suit. "Let's go over to the Tabby and have a glass of bubbly to celebrate, Robert," she said as she took his arm.

As soon as they had gone, Maggie and Hannah grabbed each other for an ecstatic dance around the kitchen. They hooted with delight, and Juan and Possum joined in with shouts and barks of glee, though Juan looked a little confused about the reason for the celebration. Hannah was in the middle of a hip roll when she noticed Bill standing in the open back door, staring open-mouthed at the four of them.

Hannah's hips froze in mid-roll, and she stared back, red-faced, at Bill. Juan began to back out of the room. But Maggie was too excited to be embarrassed. She waved Marianna's check in the air and shouted, "The Cash Floe is mine. Robert brought a new client right to our door. I've got tons of ideas for that beach house."

"Congratulations," Bill responded. "And who's this young man?"

Juan had almost succeeded in slipping away. He didn't look happy at the idea of being introduced to a police officer.

Hannah took no notice of Juan's reaction. She grabbed Bill's hand and led him out the back door. "We'll have to head over to Granny's to take a report on the attack on Althea," she said. Before Bill could ask any questions, she added, "Come on. I'll explain everything." To Maggie, she said, "After dinner, we'll come back here and enjoy the sunset. You're welcome to join us."

She was gone, dragging Bill behind her, before Maggie could reply. "Just as well," Maggie mumbled to herself. She plopped into a chair, still clutching the check. Tomorrow she would contact Salty George and give him an offer on the boat. It was time to put Cotton's death behind her and concentrate on her business, Maggie told herself firmly.

She could hear Juan pounding away on the front porch. She supposed he would work until it was time to catch the last run of the Mary Grace back to Beaufort. She walked into her office and began to pull samples in colors she thought Marianna would like. After a little more than an hour, she was satisfied with her choices.

Maggie looked out the window and stared at the sky. The sun was just beginning to set. She noticed a sailboat easing toward her dock. Probably a neighbor from the Harbour Community on the other side of the island, she decided. To get a closer look, she moved out the side door. She could hear a voice coming from the direction of her front porch. She stopped and listened. The voice grew louder. It sounded like Paul Morgan, but what would he be doing here now? She walked to the front and found Paul on his knees, inspecting Juan's work. Juan smiled. "Miss Maggie," he said, "I finish for today. Be back early tomorrow. Will look at Mr. Morgan's plans for bookcases. Okay by you?"

"As soon as you finish my porch, we'll talk about the bookcases," she answered. Then she turned to Paul, "Want to join me for a glass of wine? We can watch the sun set."

They settled onto a pair of Adirondack chairs near the dock and watched the western sky as they sipped Pinot Grigio. "Almost time to go back to my winter Shiraz," she murmured. "Will you be staying through the winter?"

"And into the summer, if the book keeps moving along. I don't have a title yet. Since my first one was *Murder in the Afternoon*, why not call this one *Murder in the Morning*? My agent doesn't like that idea, though." He turned his gaze to Maggie. "Are you planning to stay even if you don't get your design job?"

Maggie raised her glass. "This is a celebration. We have two jobs now."

Maggie lost track of time as she and Paul made small talk and night fell. Paul stood up abruptly. "Time for me to go," he said. "It's nine o'clock, and I have to finish another chapter before I call it a night."

Maggie was sorry to see him go, but she smiled brightly to hide her disappointment. "Thanks for helping me celebrate."

Paul bowed gallantly at the waist. "Delighted. See you tomorrow."

Maggie decided that she needed rest more than she needed to join Hannah and Bill for dinner. She fed Possum, filled her drinking bowl with fresh water, and got ready for bed. She opened a window to let in the cool evening air.

She had just slipped into bed when she heard a noise in the side yard, probably Bill and Hannah coming back from dinner, she thought. Possum crawled into bed next to her and began to snore softly almost immediately. But Maggie kept thinking about the murder. Every angle had been explored by the police, surely, and the locals talked of little else. Even the snowbirds who picked up the *Times* on their way through were eager to share their theories. Maggie didn't want to believe a killer was living on Seaward.

She was just drifting off to sleep when she heard a shriek. She sat straight up in bed and listened. The shrieking sound came again. This time it was so loud, it woke Possum, who jumped from the bed and growled. Could it be a cat or a wild animal in pain? She threw the covers off and pulled on a robe. Maggie grabbed Possum by the collar and crept quietly down the stairs. She tiptoed across the kitchen floor to a window and peered into the night. She could see nothing. If someone had been after Althea, would they come after her next? No one knew about the money, so what could they be after?

The howl came from just a few feet away this time. She screamed and started to run. It was then that she heard someone call her name. She flipped on the light switch in the kitchen and looked around.

Juan was halfway through the doggie door, and he was yelling at the top of his lungs. Like Hannah before him, he was stuck. "Don't shoot! Don't shoot!" he screamed. "I just wanted a place to sleep and not bother you, Miss Maggie. The ferry leave without me." Maggie crossed her arms and stared down at him. He looked up at her beseechingly. "Can I sleep on your kitchen floor?"

"You might have to sleep there for several days," Maggie snapped. "I think we'll have to either cut you out or put a pillow under your head."

It was going to be another long, exhausting night.

Ten

It took a while, but Maggie, Hannah, and Bill managed to get Juan through the doggie door without breaking out a saw. There was a lot of pulling from the front and shoving from behind—and a good bit of protesting from Juan in Spanish and broken English—but the back door remained intact.

Maggie whipped up some omelets for everyone, and then Juan was sent to a tiny guest room, which once was probably a storage area. Maggie washed and dried the omelet pan and dragged herself up the stairs to her bedroom. But she was too tense to sleep. She was staring out the window at the full moon when a glimmer caught her eye. It was too late in the year for a meteor shower. She crept out the back door and looked up. She could see sparks in the sky, probably from a campfire. Someone at the Heyward plantation had set an illegal—and potentially disastrous—campfire. Poachers perhaps? The entire island was a conservation area, and Maggie was instantly irate.

She slipped on some deck shoes and a black, hooded sweatshirt, grabbed her flashlight, and quietly walked through her gate. She sniffed the air and caught a whiff of smoke. She hurried down the road but slowed when she reached the woods. She crept through the trees and hid behind a wide, moss-covered live oak. When she peeked out, she stared, rubbed her eyes, and stared again. It couldn't possibly be...but it was.

A group of Civil War soldiers—or at least men dressed in Civil War uniforms—sat around a campfire. One of the men puffed a mournful tune through a harmonica. Maggie recognized it: an old hymn that had been sung at her uncle William's funeral, *Amazing Grace*.

Maggie stepped into the clearing, and two men swung muskets in her direction. "Don't shoot, please," she called. "It's Maggie from down the road."

"You better have a reason for being here," growled a man Maggie recognized as Hooty Simpson. Hooty's son Cal, seated on his father's left, snarled a similar warning. The shadows from the fire made hollows of their eyes, and Maggie shivered.

But another man, who turned out to be Bubba Mabry, put down his harmonica and welcomed her with a smile. "Come on over," he said. "Don't you live by Lawson Creek?"

"I saw the smoke and thought poachers had started a fire."

"The Heywards let us come over twice a year and practice our drills," Bubba explained. "We're participating in the re-enactment battle on Hilton Head, at Fort Walker. Got some new members this year. More'll be showing up tomorrow." Bubba chuckled. "I guess we shoulda spread the word better that we'd be setting fires and firing muskets. We didn't mean to scare anybody."

"I'll let the neighbors know," Maggie answered. She lingered by the fire while Bubba played old tunes on his harmonica until she began to yawn. The farewell from Hooty and Cal was much friendlier than their hello had been as Maggie set off through the woods. About halfway home, something occurred to her. All those men had on rebel uniforms, but they all wore black T-shirts under their gray jackets. That certainly wasn't right. A memory teased Maggie's brain, fluttering just out of reach, and then it came to her. Hadn't she seen someone in a black T-shirt running through the woods just after Althea had been attacked?

Maggie was just passing Althea's place, and she glanced in that direction. Out of the corner of her eye, she saw a flash at the back of the house. Or had she just imagined it? She decided she would just take a quick look to make sure Althea's animals were all right.

When a stiff breeze blew from the southwest, she could still smell the coffee bubbling over the re-enactors' campfire. There had probably been real rebels hiding in these woods when Sherman's Army came through Beaufort, Maggie supposed.

Althea's house was dark, and Maggie walked up to the front stoop and looked around. The only sound she heard came from palmetto branches moving in the breeze.

Maggie turned the doorknob, and the door swung open. She hesitated briefly, remembering the attack on Althea, and then walked inside. She flicked on the flashlight and gasped. The place had been trashed. Every knick-knack had been thrown from its shelf; stuffing had been torn from the chairs and the sofa. Maggie picked her way carefully through the mess and into Althea's kitchen. Blue Willow plates and cups had been reduced to shards of glass scattered across the floor.

Maggie's first instinct was to clean up the mess, but she realized that would be useless. Everywhere she turned, there was only rubble.

In the bedroom, the mattress had been dragged onto the floor and slashed, a chest had been overturned, and even boards in the floor had been smashed. Maggie knelt to get a closer look, shining her flashlight into the holes in the floor, and something white caught her eye. She snatched it up and her hand flew to her mouth. It was an envelope with her name on it. She stuffed it into her pocket and looked around, but she saw nothing else in the mess that would be of any particular interest to anyone.

Then she heard the front door squeak. Was someone coming in or sneaking out? She plastered herself against a wall and crept toward the bedroom door. Standing in the light of the moon was an apparition in a Civil War uniform. But this was no ghost. He pushed back his floppy, brown hat and moonlight illuminated his face. She recognized him—Sherman Pritchard—and breathed a sigh of relief. Underneath a butternut-colored jacket with shiny brass buttons, he wore a black T-shirt. A haversack hung across his chest.

Maggie stepped out of the bedroom. Sherman jumped, and then he recognized her and grinned. She shone her flashlight onto his face and wondered how long he had been in the house.

"What are you doing here in the middle of the night?" she demanded.

He shielded his eyes from the flashlight's glare. "I could ask you the same thing."

"I'm checking on Althea's animals," Maggie snapped. "She's staying at Granny's and asked me to keep an eye on things. I thought Sadie might have come home. She wasn't here this afternoon." She gave Sherman a hard stare. "And you?"

Sherman poked out his bottom lip, looking like a petulant child, and for a minute Maggie thought he might tell her it was none of her business. "I was following you," he said. "I wanted to talk to you about the attack on Althea. I got the police report, and it named you as a witness." Sherman threw out his chest and stood as tall as he could. "I am a journalist, you know."

"I have nothing to say about that, Sherm," Maggie answered flatly.

He nodded, as if this was exactly the answer he expected, and took a long look around at the wreckage. "Wish I knew what kind of sicko would tear up a place like this. Senseless." He shook his head sadly. "Well, I have to get back to my tent. We're practicing with the muskets all weekend. I told Bill Johnson what we're doing over there, but I don't know if he'll be as lenient as Hammond." Sherman eyed Maggie hopefully. "I hope we get a break in Cotton's case soon. I'd like to report that Bill has some leads. Does he?" When Maggie didn't answer, Sherman added, "You probably better let Bill tell Althea about this. Looks like she lost just about everything."

Sherman tipped his floppy hat in Maggie's direction. "Good evening," he said, but he didn't move. Maggie realized he wanted her to leave first. Maybe that meant that he had been the one who had trashed the place and he hadn't found what he was looking for. If that was what he wanted, she would oblige. She stepped past him and out the door. He could stay there until daylight and not find the note she had in her pocket, if that's what he was looking for.

When she reached her own back door, it occurred to her that she had not asked him about the black T-shirts.

Maggie plodded into the house and tiptoed upstairs to bed, trying not to disturb anyone. Possum had waited up, and she jumped into bed the minute Maggie lay down.

Maggie pulled out the note and examined the envelope. There was no stamp, no postmark. She opened the envelope with trembling fingers and unfolded the note. It was from Cotton. Since he had not mailed it, Maggie assumed he had meant to give it to her personally. Did Althea know about this? Probably not. She would have handed it over before now.

Maggie read what Cotton had scrawled across the page, and her eyes filled with tears.

Dear Miss Maggie:
    I am sending you a package. Keep it for me. I am moving to Savannah to help a friend start his business. I'll explain when I come back.
Sincerely,

Cotton

Maggie wiped the tears away and lay back on her pillow. Possum sighed in her sleep, and Maggie closed her eyes. She dreamed of Cotton that night. He was trying to tell her something, but she couldn't understand what he was saying.

A bell clanged somewhere, causing Maggie to wake with a start. She sat straight up in bed before she realized it was just her alarm clock going off. It was 9:22 A.M. Maggie grabbed her bedside phone, dialed, and snuggled back under the covers with the phone pressed to her ear.

"Thought you would have called before now," Robert said. "You able to work with Marianna? She's a great lady."

"I agree," Maggie answered. "I would have called sooner, but it was a long night. I have a question for you: Have you seen a bunch of people wearing black T-shirts in the last few days? Someone in black knocked Althea in the head yesterday. She's okay," Maggie added quickly, when she heard a gasp on his end of the line. "I just wondered if one of those re-enactor guys might have had something to do with it."

Maggie heard Robert expel a long breath. "You stay out of it," he said sternly. "Haven't I told you to stay out of trouble? Bill Johnson is being paid to investigate crimes. Not that he's doing much investigating since he met your friend Hannah."

"I just wanted to know..."

"I hope we see everybody on the island wearing a black T-shirt," Robert interrupted. "Those shirts are the ones I sell at the marina. Just started carrying them. I gave a box to those crazy re-enactors, and I had to send the rest back because the silkscreen shop printed the 'Bluff' in Palmetto Bluff Marina with one f. B-l-u-f, for godsakes!"

Robert paused, probably trying to calm down, Maggie figured.

"Anyway," he continued, "Jim says you all have got everything under control for the oyster roast and wine-tasting. We've ordered everything, and I got the tables. We're still taking reservations. It's going to be a real shindig!"

"Too bad you won't have any T-shirts to sell," Maggie said with a giggle.

"I'm gonna ignore that," Robert huffed. "Oh, by the way, I found a flare gun for you. I'll give it to you tonight."

"Tonight?"

"Meet us at the Bayview Grill after your meeting with Chandler. What do you say?" He didn't wait for Maggie to answer. "Gotta go." Just before he put down the phone, he added, "Quit nosing around in this murder business. I don't want to see you get hurt."

Maggie had every intention of heeding her friend's advice. She fingered Cotton's note, wondering what she would do with it. She'd put it with the money and keep her mouth shut, she decided. When Bill caught the killer—*if* he caught the killer—she would see if the money or the note had any bearing on the case. If so, she'd hand them over.

She swung her legs out of the bed, but before her feet had hit the floor, the phone rang. Maggie reached for it, but it stopped ringing almost immediately. Hannah yelled from downstairs. "Someone named Maude from the Heyward Plantation wants us to come over. Want to pick up?"

Maggie snatched up the phone with a smile on her face. She pulled it back an inch or so away from her ear when Maude boomed a greeting. "Where you been hidin' yourself?" Maude demanded. "Get over here and have some lunch. I want to meet your Rosemont friend and catch up with what's been goin' on with you."

"Be there in a few," Maggie said. She didn't mention that she was just getting up. Maude, who was up and working before the crack of dawn every morning, would have been horrified.

Juan was waiting for instructions when Maggie came downstairs, and it took a few minutes to persuade Hannah that even though Maude wasn't a potential client, she was a person worth getting to know. Maggie wanted to get moving because she wanted to leave

125

the plantation in plenty of time to put a deposit on her boat before she met Robert at the Bayou Grill. Hannah wanted to change from shorts into a skirt for the visit and put on some makeup, and Maggie half-dragged her out of the house.

They climbed into a golf cart Robert had loaned Maggie. It wouldn't go more than fifteen or twenty miles an hour, but it was ideal for getting around the tiny island.

As they putted toward the plantation, Maggie reflected on her new business' solid start, and she felt that her life was finally falling into place.

When she pulled the cart into the plantation's driveway, she heard Hannah whistle.

"Did Paramount film *Gone with the Wind* here?" Hannah asked in awe. "Those are the most perfect white columns I've ever seen."

Maggie just laughed. She remembered her own similar reaction when she first saw the Heywards' home. She parked the cart by a wide staircase leading to the front door. Before she and Hannah were halfway up the steps, Maude clomped out of the front door waving a dishtowel.

One look at Maude and anyone could tell that she was an excellent cook—and that she didn't skimp on portions for anyone, including herself. She was short and very wide. Maggie thought Maude must have been about sixty or sixty-five. Her hair had gone white, but her eyes were still a clear and vivid blue. Her face was smooth except for deep laugh lines around her eyes and mouth.

As soon as Maggie was within reach, she took Maude's hands. "I've missed you," she said, and Maude beamed.

"We're having cold green tomato soup for lunch," Maude announced proudly. "I made it this morning. You young'uns are too skinny. I'll give you both a slab of cornbread and a big dollop of sour cream on the soup. I think I got some walnut pound cake left from last night, too."

126

"It's not even noon yet!" Hannah protested.

But Maude hustled them into the kitchen, sat them down at the table, and plopped an alarming amount of food in front of them. It was clear to both women they were expected to clean their plates, and Hannah looked a little panicky, but the first spoonful of Maude's soup put a smile on her face.

Maude filled a plate and bowl for herself and eased herself into a chair.

Even the tea was exceptional in Maude's kitchen. The leaves grew on bushes at the plantation. John had said they were special types of camellia bushes.

While the three women ate, Maude quizzed Hannah about her background. Hannah was well aware that family lineage was important information to Southerners, and she answered Maude's questions with good humor.

"My father was Episcopalian, but my mother went to First Baptist in Rosemont," Hannah said.

Maude nodded her approval of the Baptist connection, and then her smile faded. "I was just thinking what happened at Pastor Kelly's church in Ruffin," she said. "That place done burned down twice since it was put up in 1789. The altar made it through both fires, but they had to replace the pews. Hard, uncomfortable pews made of wood with no paddin'. But the preacher wanted the seats exactly the same as they was before the fire." Maude leaned close to Maggie and said confidentially, "He was prob'ly worried if folks got comfortable, they might fall asleep during one of his long sermons. Anyway, the only person who could do the job right was Cotton."

Maude sighed deeply, and her massive bosom strained against her flowered housedress.

"Did the pastor pay Cotton well for his work?" Maggie asked.

"Them new people in Beaufort gave the money for the church to be restored. Chandler Morris and his sister."

"They're new here?" Hannah interrupted. "I thought they'd been here a while."

"Only been here ten years," Maude answered emphatically. "Guess they didn't know what to do with all that money they made buildin' apartments." Maude wrinkled her nose in distaste. "Come down here to save us from ourselves, I reckon. But the church gave the money to Cotton, and he fixed them pews good as new. Except he made 'em look old, like they'd always been there. He was the best carpenter this side of heaven, and that's a fact." Maude huffed indignantly. "I bet that no-good wife took all that church money when she divorced him and went out West."

"Do you know how much it was? The money?"

Maude shook her head mournfully. "Don't seem like it matters no more. You could ask Pastor Kelly, I guess." She looked up at Maggie with an indignant expression. "You reckon somebody killed Cotton for that money?"

"Anything is possible," Maggie said carefully.

Hannah savored another spoonful of green tomato soup. "We'll pass this information on to Bill. He is doing a thorough investigation, you know."

Hannah looked so proud, Maggie didn't have the heart to disagree, but she was certain that Bill had no idea who the murderer was. She glanced at a round-faced, Victorian station clock at the end of the breakfast nook. It was an amazing piece, and Maggie stared at it with a touch of envy. Then she noticed the time.

"My goodness," she exclaimed. "We've got to go. The Mary Grace will be at the dock in twenty minutes."

"But you didn't even taste the walnut cake," Maude protested. "Here, let me wrap you up some to take with you."

By the time Hannah and Maggie got to Markley Marina, the Mary Grace was pulling into her berth. The ferry looked deserted. Maggie spotted Randy cleaning seats. When the ferry started to pull away from the dock, Hannah headed for the shelter inside to keep her hair tidy, and she mumbled something about putting on her face before she saw Bill. Maggie decided this would be the perfect time to have that talk she had been planning with Randy.

Maggie popped her head into the wheelhouse. "I saw you going off course a few days ago," she remarked. "What was the problem?"

Randy concentrated on his job and ignored her.

She tried again. "There's got to be a reason you're never on schedule. Sometimes you're early, and sometimes you're late. How come?"

Randy didn't look up. "Dianne is taking a few days off. Maybe when she comes back to work, we can get on a better schedule."

Maggie decided not to press the issue. Maybe Randy and Dianne were having marital problems. That would certainly make it hard to concentrate on a schedule.

"Listen, Randy, I'm curious about something," she said. "Were there any strange people on the Mary Grace the night Cotton was killed? You've probably talked to Bill about that by now, right?"

"He hasn't asked." Randy looked up at Maggie for the first time during their conversation. "There was a woman on the afternoon run who didn't look familiar. I'm not sure she'd ever been to Seaward. Tall, red hair, well dressed for this neck of the woods. I meant to ask her who she was going to see, but we had a boat load and we were running late. Didn't see her come back on the final run that night, come to think of it."

The woman Randy described sounded a lot like the woman she and Hannah had seen in the bathroom at the Ribaut Inn. The redhead had walked out of a stall while Maggie and Hannah were talking. Maggie tried to remember what they had said. She thought it was something about Cotton—or had they been talking about Chandler Morris? She'd have to ask Hannah.

When Hannah and Maggie got off the Mary Grace, Salty George was standing on the dock beside the Cash Floe with a big grin on his face. "I got you a better price than I thought. He's going to let you have her without a down payment. Just need to get the title transferred and send him a monthly check."

"I brought a check with me," Maggie said. "Where is he? Are you going to take it to him? I've never had to handle a transaction like this before."

Salty George gave Maggie a reassuring pat. "Don't worry. He won't come do a repo on you. He left this morning for Nova Scotia. I'll make sure you get it all done right. Just relax and enjoy your new boat. I'm goin' to the fishing tournament on Edisto next week. When I get back, I'll check on you. Just practice what I taught you."

Salty George gave Maggie another grin and disappeared around the side of the Beaufort marina.

Maggie and Hannah walked together toward the Ribaut Inn. The tourists were thinning out, but there were still a few on the street. The sky was already going dark.

"It's getting dark so early these days," Maggie commented.

Hannah grunted a response. She took a silver compact from her purse and powdered her nose. Maggie asked what she could remember about their conversation in the Ribaut Inn restroom, but Hannah didn't seem particularly interested. Maggie resolved to tell Bill about the redheaded woman at dinner. She would let him decide if any of this information mattered.

She opened the door to the Inn, strolled into the lobby, and looked around.

An elevator door was just closing. Standing inside was the tall, redheaded woman.

Maggie watched the buttons above the door light up as the elevator ascended.

It stopped on the third floor.

Eleven

Maggie sent Hannah into the meeting and ran for the stairs. She took them two at a time. By the time she had reached the third floor, the woman had disappeared.

Maggie had no idea which room the woman had gone into. She caught her breath and wondered if she could convince Chandler to let her look at the names of the people who had checked into rooms on the third floor in the last few days.

Slowly, she walked back down the stairs and into the meeting, where Hannah and Chandler were talking over decorating plans. Hannah gave Maggie an icy look. Chandler handed Maggie a sheet of paper upon which he had scratched some notes.

"I have ideas for the outside balconies that face the courtyard," he said.

Maggie looked over the notes with a sigh of relief. Chandler wanted some modifications to their plans, but he hadn't rejected them.

"We'll be happy to do this," she said. "We'll report back in about two weeks. That will give us time to order fabric and come up with a firm timeframe for you." She gave Chandler a grateful smile. "Thanks for sending Juan, by the way. He's finishing my porch, and I'll help him line up some other jobs on Seaward."

"Fine boy," Chandler answered. "He has family in Mexico, and he hopes to bring them here next year. Two years ago, he was picking tomatoes and now he's doing much better. Got his green card, too. Take good care of him, Maggie." He stood to signal the meeting was over. "I wish I could join you all tonight, but I have a meeting in Charleston tomorrow at nine." He picked up his briefcase and walked through a door at the back of his office. He left so abruptly, Maggie didn't have a chance to ask about his third-floor guests.

Well, everyone was waiting for them at the restaurant, Maggie told herself, and anyway, hadn't she learned her lesson last year when that student was killed and she poked her nose in? She had almost followed him to the grave.

Maggie and Hannah strolled to the Bay View Grill in silence. Hannah was still miffed about Maggie's disappearing act.

Bill was waiting at a table, and his eyes lit up when Hannah sashayed in. Jim was there, too, having wrangled a few hours off. Maggie wondered if Robert was trying to play matchmaker.

She walked toward Jim, intending to give him a peck on the cheek, but she stumbled over a package by his chair.

"I had to buy a bottle of bleach," he explained. "I've been experimenting with mustard-based sauces, and I've made quite a mess on three white smocks."

Maggie skipped the kiss and took a seat. "We should have a bunch of different sauces, don't you think? Have you decided on any particular flavor combinations?"

"Simple. Most visitors will want something they can duplicate. The mustard sauce is Dijon, honey, horseradish, and a little Worcestershire. Haven't decided what I'll put in the catsup sauce. I know it'll have horseradish, though."

Maggie glanced down at the package at Jim's feet. "I hope you haven't put bleach in any of your sauces," she said lightly.

"What? Don't you think bleach would give our oysters a unique taste?" he answered with a laugh.

Maggie and Jim talked about their plans and sipped white wine while the table filled up around them. When everyone was in place, Robert clinked his glass with his spoon. All eyes turned his way. "Marianna is moving to Seaward," he announced.

Marianna raised her glass, and the others followed suit. "My offer was accepted," she said. "I have a new house and a great design team."

Maggie waited for the cheers to die down. Then she turned to Marianna. "Let's meet next week at the house," she said. "Hannah and I already have ideas you're going to love."

Conversation was brisk and cheerful, and the food and wine were delicious.

Near the end of the evening, Robert presented Maggie with a new flare gun and flares, prompting giggles and guffaws from those who knew the story of her rescue. "It's very lightweight," he told her, "and easily fired, once you flip off the safety mechanism." He showed her how to load the gun and how to operate the trigger. "But, remember," he cautioned, "even the best-made flare guns can be dangerous. Always look away before you fire to protect your eyes, and hold the gun away from your body. The sparks can catch your clothes on fire, and there's a liquid—some sort of fuel—in the thing, I'm told, that sticks to the skin and burns like molten lava."

When it was time to head home, Maggie happily announced that she had made the first payment on her boat and would not be taking the ferry anymore. Bill, Hannah, and Jim wanted to ride back to Seaward on the Cash Floe. Robert and Marianna preferred to wait for the Mary Grace—not that they doubted Maggie's skills at the helm, Robert quickly assured her with a wicked grin.

Jim took Maggie's arm as they walked toward the marina, and she felt a surge of affection for him. He had been great fun that evening, and during their conversation, she had learned that they had similar interests.

Bill and Maggie began preparations to take the Cash Floe out of her slip. When Maggie looked around, she couldn't see Jim anywhere. "How odd," she murmured to no one in particular. "He said he wanted to ride with us."

Maggie scanned the area around the water, trying to catch sight of him. Instead, she saw a tall redhead step briefly under a light on the path near the marina. Maggie couldn't see her face, so she couldn't be sure it was the same woman from the Inn. The woman strolled toward the marina. And then Maggie caught sight of Jim, walking in the same direction.

He turned and threw Maggie a kiss before he walked out of sight.

"What was that about?" Hannah asked. "I thought he was riding back with us."

Maggie felt let down but didn't want Hannah to know, so she lifted her shoulders and dropped them. "I thought so, too. Then he goes after this woman we saw at the Inn, the redhead. Either she works there or she's staying in a room on the third floor."

"There are some good-looking chicks at the Inn," Bill said. When he saw the stormy look in Hannah's eyes, he added quickly, "Not as pretty as you, of course."

Maggie concentrated on the Cash Floe and pushed Jim and the redhead from her mind. She remembered to stash Robert's new flare contraption under a seat on the boat.

Bill helped Maggie stow seat cushions away when they had docked on Seaward. "Nice boat, Maggie," he said. "She floats through the water like a slick mermaid. You're going to be glad you got this boat this winter. The Mary Grace may not be running much longer."

Maggie grunted in disgust. "You're right. They're never on time."

Bill grabbed Hannah's hand and headed for the cottage. Maggie walked behind. As she came into the yard, she heard voices. Paul, Juan, and Althea were waiting on her porch. Althea held a wriggling piglet in her arms.

"I came to tell you bye," Althea said. "I'm scared to stay here. Whoever ripped my cottage apart might come back. Sallie Jo and

Granny'll take care of my animals, the ones I didn't give away, and I'll take a few with me. I'll be in Port Royal. Maybe you can come visit." Althea thrust the piglet into Maggie's arms. "This is for you."

Maggie opened her mouth to protest, but she saw the proud look on Althea's face.

"It's a present," Althea said in the same tone she might have used if she had given a diamond necklace. "Granny said she'd help you look after it." Althea gave Maggie a pitying look. "You never raised pigs, so you'll need some guidance."

The piglet was not nearly as happy with the arrangement as Althea, and Maggie had to wrap her arms around the little fellow's chubby middle. "Thank you very much," she said, hoping she sounded sincere.

"Where will you go?" Bill asked.

"I got a job re-covering a couch for Mr. Todd in Port Royal. I'll stay at a cheap little motel near there. I'm not gonna pay rent on this dump over here anymore."

"I'll be glad to take over your lease," Hannah said eagerly.

Maggie stared at her in astonishment.

"It'll be perfect until I find a more permanent place," Hannah explained. "Maggie and I are getting our business off the ground, and I can't mooch off her forever. I'm sorry you have to leave, Althea, but no one will bother me, I'm sure. Let's look at the place tomorrow and see what we can do." She grabbed Bill's hand and pulled him into Maggie's cottage.

It suddenly dawned on Maggie what Hannah was up to. She would turn it into a showplace, a wonderful way to advertise their decorating talents.

"Smart move," Maggie called after her friend.

"Well, that be settled. That's good," Althea said, but she looked like she might cry.

Maggie touched her shoulder. "Althea, are you sure you want to do this?"

Althea nodded. "Wreckin' my house was just the last straw. I didn't really want to stay there without my Cotton anyway. Too many memories."

Maggie turned her attention back to the piglet, still squirming in her arms. "What do I do with this guy?"

Althea plucked him from Maggie's grasp. "I'll take him to Granny's tonight, since you don't have a place for him built. She'll bring him back tomorrow and tell you what he needs."

"But...but..." Maggie's mind raced, trying to think of a way to reject the present without hurting Althea's feelings. "Possum might be upset if I have another pet. Maybe I can buy pig food and let the little fella come for visits. That way, Granny gets to keep him, but I can help take care of him."

"Well, you can talk to Granny about it," Althea said, looking doubtful, "but she's pretty set in her ways on certain things."

Maggie could hear the piglet squealing long after Althea had disappeared into the dark.

When Maggie turned around, she saw that everyone had left the porch but Paul. The bright harvest moon painted a shimmering path across Lawson Creek.

Maggie took one last look in the direction Althea had gone. "It's been an exciting day," she commented wryly as she took a seat near Paul.

"I tried to catch you before you went to Beaufort," he said. "Sorry I didn't make it. Everybody at the Red Eye said you got the job you were after and bought a boat."

Maggie nodded. "My life is coming together. How's the book coming?"

Paul frowned. "Don't ask. Too many new characters popping up." He paused, and Maggie wondered what was on his mind. He didn't make her wait long. "Would you join me for dinner tomorrow night? Sometimes if I get away from writing for a few hours, I can recharge my creative batteries."

"That happens to me when I'm planning a new design for a large project. Must be part of the creative process. Want to take my boat and go over to Edisto? There's a seafood shack on the waterway that most people pass by. It looks grubby, but they've got the best crab cakes on the East Coast. The cook uses less filler and lots of crab. We could go about four and have a great ride down the Beaufort River."

"I'll be here," he said. "See you tomorrow." Before Maggie could reply, he leaned over and kissed her on the mouth. "Take care," he said as he walked away.

Maggie stood in a daze. She thought she could hear bells ringing in the distance. *Never had that reaction to a kiss before*, she thought. She hummed a little tune as she turned to go inside.

Bill and Hannah ran through the door at that moment, nearly bowling her over. Bill was shouting into his cell phone. So that's where the ringing sound had come from, Maggie realized. That certainly took some of the romance out of the situation.

Bill pushed an arm into his Izod jacket and updated Maggie breathlessly. "There's been an emergency at the marina in town. Police boat on the way to pick me up."

"What happened?"

"A woman was either pushed into the river or fell off the boat." He gave Hannah a quick kiss. "I'll call you later."

Bill ran out of the yard just as Jim strolled in. He watched Bill race away, then turned to greet Maggie. "Great, you're still awake. I wanted to apologize for not riding over with you. I left my bleach in the restaurant and had to go back and get it. Can't show up for work tomorrow in a smock with yellow stains all over it. Anyway, I wanted to tell you that I had a great time tonight."

Out of the corner of her eye, Maggie saw Hannah slip quietly into the house. *She has high hopes for a romance between Jim and me,* Maggie thought, *and maybe I do, too.*

Jim pointed in the direction Bill had run. "Where's he off to in such a hurry?"

"We heard someone drowned at the dock," Maggie answered. "Did you see anything?"

Jim shook his head. "I guess I left before all the excitement. Caught a ride with Bubba. He brought his boat over and plans to camp out with the rest of those Civil War nuts."

Without warning, Jim pulled Maggie to him and kissed her forcefully on the lips.

Then he, too, disappeared into the night. "See you tomorrow," he called back to her.

Maggie stood still for a minute and listened carefully. Nope, no bells this time—not even a cell phone ringing.

Hannah had put on her sleepy pants and curled up on a down-filled chair. At last, the two friends had time to talk.

"Next week, we'll clean out Althea's house and go over to Island Cottages in Charleston," Maggie said. "I've seen a great sleigh bed there."

"I'd like to have plantation shutters on the window. I can't remember the scale. Would those windows be too small for that, do you think? Let's remember to measure them tomorrow."

"I may not have time tomorrow," Maggie said. "I have to convince Granny that I do not need one of Alberta's baby pigs. Can you imagine a pigsty in my back yard? We need to do a little work for Caroline at the Rosemont firm, too. And—oh, yes—I'm going to Edisto for an early dinner with Paul. He and I had a great time on the porch tonight." Maggie blushed a little, and Hannah sat up straight, waiting for a report.

When Maggie didn't elaborate, Hannah remarked, "I guess Jim blew it, huh?"

"Well, he did come by to apologize for leaving us like that." Maggie tapped her forehead, trying to remember what else she needed to take care of the next day. "Oh, I promised Salty George I'd change the title on my boat. I'll check with Robert on that. I'd better make a list before I forget something."

Maggie picked up a Parker pen and a notepad she kept on top of a stained rattan table.

"Are you sleepy?" Hannah asked.

Maggie shook her head as she scribbled out her to-do list.

"Good," Hannah said. "Let's go over to measure those windows right now. Bring that pad and pen."

"It's past one o'clock in the morning," Maggie protested. "What if somebody sees us wandering around over there this late?"

"I'll just tell them Bill asked me to check and make sure the house is locked." Hannah snapped her fingers. "Which reminds me: I have to get some locks for that place. There's no way to lock the windows, which is why it was easy for someone to break in there and trash everything. Bill thinks it was someone who knew that Cotton had given Althea some money."

Hannah was already pulling on her jacket, so Maggie grabbed her sweatshirt. The nights were getting cooler now, but the lowcountry was still warmer than other parts of the state this time of year. Maggie zipped up her sweatshirt and pulled up the hood. It only took a few minutes for the women to walk to the cottage.

"Let's go in the back way in case someone is lurking around," Maggie whispered.

Hannah grunted her assent. "Okay, but I don't think we have anything to worry about. If someone was looking for Althea's money, they found out it's not here."

They slipped around the house and tiptoed up the back steps. They slowly opened the door and stepped into the kitchen. It was dark and deathly still inside the house, and Maggie shivered. She pulled out her flashlight. Hannah, on the other hand, didn't seem even a little nervous.

"Here, hold the pen and paper," Maggie instructed. "Make sure you write down the measurements right this time." Maggie giggled. "Remember the fiasco we had with Suzanne Smith's brocade curtains?"

"You know she changed the measurements on us because her husband didn't want to pay full price. Remember? He told her a man's home was his castle, but he wasn't willing to pay enough to make it look like a palace."

Maggie forgot her nervousness, and both women howled with laughter. Hannah held a broken chair steady against the wall while Maggie climbed up, trying to stop laughing long enough to hold the tape measure straight. She read out the width and length to Hannah.

Neither woman saw the man who stepped into the doorway behind them.

Then Maggie glanced over Hannah's shoulder and screamed. Hannah was so startled, she let go of the rickety chair, causing Maggie to tumble to the floor. Hannah threw up her hands. "Please don't shoot!" she yelled.

Juan stepped from the shadows into the moonlight.

"Oh, Miss Hannah, I did not mean to scare you," he said. "Are you okay, Miss Maggie?"

Juan flipped a wall switch, and light flooded the room. "I told Miss Althea I would keep an eye on this place. I thought sleeping here would be the best way."

Maggie grumbled under her breath as she stood up and dusted herself off. "Tell the truth, Juan," she said. "You don't have a place to stay, do you? Last night you were at my house. Tonight you show up here."

Juan dropped his head.

"Well, I'm glad you're here," Maggie said. "Help us measure these windows. And when we're done, you can come back to my house and sleep in that back room, at least until you finish the porch. Then we'll see what we can do about finding something more permanent. Why didn't you tell me?"

Juan didn't look up. "I would get in trouble with Dianne and Randy. They want me to always be helping them. I told them Mr. Morris sent me here. Will you talk to them?"

"They need more than a carpenter for their dirty boat," Maggie huffed. "I'll call them tomorrow."

"I saw a ladder at the side of the house," Juan said. "I will get it so I can measure the windows for you."

Juan ran to get the ladder. While Hannah was waiting, she pulled her cell phone out of her pocket and checked her messages. "Bill called," she said. "I'll call him back if you want to know what happened."

Maggie nodded. "You call while Juan and I measure."

Juan set the ladder at each window in turn, and he and Maggie completed the measurements quickly.

Hannah put her phone back in her pocket, and her hands were shaking. She looked scared to death.

"What?" Maggie demanded.

"A woman was pushed off the dock into the Beaufort River a few minutes before the Mary Grace arrived. She hasn't been identified yet, but Bill says she had blond hair and is about the same height and weight as you, Maggie. But she wasn't as lucky as you were. She drowned before anyone could reach her."

Twelve

Maggie sat at her kitchen table with Bill and Hannah. In the distance, they could hear Juan banging his hammer. "Mistaken identity," Maggie said. "You think I was pushed into the Beaufort River because I looked like someone the killer wanted to…" She covered her face with her hands and shuddered.

Bill poured half and half into the coffee cup in front of him. "The divers are still searching for I.D. If she had a purse, it probably sunk to the bottom. You know how heavy a purse can be."

His attempt at levity earned him doleful glances from the women. Maggie knew this woman fit into the investigation of Cotton's death somehow, even if Bill didn't, and that the killer was still in the area.

"You're positive she wasn't a redhead?" Maggie asked.

Hannah raised her eyebrows. "What difference does that make?"

"Last night, Jim told me he wanted to retrieve his bleach from the restaurant, but then I thought he went inside the store to talk to the woman I see every time we go to the mainland. He seemed to be following her." Maggie shook her head in frustration. "It's very confusing."

"That could be Stella Banks," Bill said. "I've seen Jim out with her a few times. He wasn't around the dock when we recovered the body. Didn't Hannah tell me he came by here after he got back to Seaward last night?"

"Yes, he came by. I don't remember seeing the bottle of bleach," Maggie answered.

"Would you carry a bottle of bleach to a woman's house if you wanted to make some smooth moves?" Bill retorted.

This time, Maggie and Hannah laughed.

Maggie thought of her date with Paul coming up that afternoon, and she told herself it was good that Jim was seeing Stella. But she felt a twinge of jealousy, just the same.

Bill said his goodbyes and headed back to the crime scene.

Maggie and Hannah stared at the to-do list in front of them on the table.

"What do we do first?" Hannah asked.

"Order the materials for the spreads and quilts at Ribaut Inn. We've got to get that done first. Let's talk to Althea about making them for us. That way, we can design the coverlet details. I've seen some of her work. She's a true seamstress. Then call Caroline with the information she wants at Rosemont Interiors and give the company a call about those shutters for your new place."

"Is it silly to give the place a name? I want to call it Rose Cottage. I can picture lots of beautiful, old-fashioned roses blooming around the place."

Maggie smiled. "It's not silly at all. I've been toying with the idea of calling this place Palmetto Grove. There are more palmetto trees than live oaks in the yard." She glanced out the window at the palmettos in the back yard. The image of a pigsty cluttering that view reminded Maggie of another important task. "Oh, and I have to go make a polite refusal to the gift of a pig. You want to start on the calls while I take care of that? I'll take Possum with me. When Granny sees that Possum will want to make a snack of that little porker, she won't be so eager to give it to me—I hope." She stood up and called Possum. "Come on, girl, let's go see Granny Jones."

Hannah picked up the phone. Maggie chuckled when she heard Hannah calling the plantation shutter company first.

Maggie slid Possum's favorite brown leather leash around the dog's neck, and they strolled up the road toward Granny's house. When Possum caught sight of Granny, rocking on the front porch, she strained to get off her leash. Dickie kept Granny supplied with scraps and bones from the Red Eye's restaurant, and Granny was always eager to share them with Possum whenever she and Maggie came to visit.

Granny didn't give Possum her usual friendly greeting, though, and Possum lay down at the edge of the porch and sulked. Granny sat solemnly with her hands folded in her lap. Arthritis and hard work had gnarled and swollen the old woman's knuckles, but she still chopped her own wood and grew much of her own produce. "Bad things goin' on in our neck of the woods," Granny said as Maggie sat in a rocker next to her.

Maggie caught a whiff of veggie soup, which she knew would be simmering on a wood stove in the kitchen next to the electric range that Granny never touched. The Heywards had installed the range last Christmas. Sallie Jo had used it a few times, and she had managed to get Granny interested in learning to bake bread in it. But Sallie Jo was too pregnant now to carry through with the lessons—which gave Maggie an idea.

"I tell you what," Maggie said. "I'll teach you to make breads, pies, and cakes in that new oven of yours if you'll keep the pig that Althea wanted to give me."

Granny sniffed. "What makes you think you would get one of those little piggies? They mine to give, and not Althea's. Little Lavender thinks he's gettin' one, too, but he's been studyin' too much about pigs sniffin' out something in the woods. Says he can charge a bunch of money for food with some fancy mushroom in it." Granny rocked harder, causing Maggie to worry that she might accidentally catapult herself from the chair. "I never heard of such a thing. He's not gettin' my pig to let loose in the woods. Them wild boars would get that little pig for sure."

Granny shot Maggie a sly look, and her rocking slowed. "'Course, maybe I'm being too hasty. Maybe you should have one of those pigs. Might be good for you to learn a little bit about raisin' swine. You got a lot of book learnin', but you don't know much about important stuff like raisin' pigs and cannin' vegetables."

Maggie caught her breath. "I'll bet a pig could root under my fence and run away. Not to mention what Possum would do if she thought a little pig was going to eat her food."

"Well," Granny said, "I guess if you got that little carpenter of yours to build me a proper sty, and if you agreed to help me feed these little fellers, I guess that might be fair."

"You've got a deal," Maggie said quickly. "Now, what's for lunch? Do I get some of that soup I smell?"

Maggie followed Granny into the kitchen. Possum took her place under the table, waiting for something delicious to fall to the floor. Granny put some corn fritters in a cast iron skillet to fry. In no time flat, Granny was serving Maggie lunch on yellow, blue, and green Fiestaware she had salvaged from Althea's wrecked cottage.

Granny fingered a plate, nicked on the edge, and clucked her tongue over the horror of recent events.

"Do you think we could all be killed in our beds?" she asked abruptly, causing Maggie to put down her soupspoon and examine the old woman's face. Granny sounded genuinely scared, and not much had ever scared Granny. "Them people that come through on the boats coulda killed Cotton, but I don't think they'd of stayed to do more damage. I'm bettin' them crazy Civil War actors had a few homebrews—that stuff is pretty strong for them that's not used to it—and wrecked Althea's place."

Maggie patted Granny's hand. "There's no proof that they've done anything except play soldier."

"Well, Althea was ready to move anyway. The place wadn't good for her after Cotton died." Granny sighed sorrowfully. "Say, about that new builder of yours: Is he any good? Won't be as good as Cotton, I'll wager." Granny leaned close and lowered her voice as if she was imparting a shameful secret. "He's not American, you know. If

I was you, I'd check with Dianne and Randy. They seem to know all them workers from Mexico. They can tell you is he trustworthy." Her eyes bored into Maggie's. "He could even be the killer. We don't know who his family is."

Maggie looked away quickly so Granny couldn't see that she was fighting back a grin. "I had planned to talk to Randy today, if I can catch him at the ferry landing. I'll ask him about Juan. But if it'll make you feel any better, the owner of the Ribaut Inn says Juan is a good kid and a talented carpenter. He'll build the sty for your pigs, and you'll get to know him. That'll set your mind at ease, I'm sure."

When Maggie had drained her bowl and eaten more fritters than one woman should be able to eat, she and Possum set out on the path to Markley's Landing. The trip took longer than it should have because Possum stopped to smell every bush and bark at every squirrel.

Possum stuck her nose in a clump of grass, and Maggie smelled a sweet scent in the air. She bent to examine the grass Possum was snuffling, and saw a discarded bouquet of magenta and white flowers on the ground. Stargazer lilies. It looked like someone had trampled them. Whoever had been carrying them might have discovered their dirty little secret: Their stamens stained everything they touched. She had smelled them recently somewhere—was it at Althea's house? Maggie pulled Possum away. She didn't want Possum's nose stained yellow.

By the time Maggie had dragged the Lab to the dock, she found the Mary Grace had come and gone already. The ferry had been fifteen minutes early. Maggie was fuming; she had wanted to talk to Randy. She absently watched three women walk off the dock, carrying groceries and flowers they had probably bought at the flea market in Charleston. Althea had told her the flea market sold bunches of flowers at discounted prices. "I guess that's where those lilies came from," Maggie told Possum as she scratched behind the dog's ears. "Somebody dropped them on the path from the dock."

She shrugged off her failed attempt to catch Randy and led Possum back toward their home. She wanted plenty of time to get ready for her date with Paul.

Hannah was still talking on the phone when Maggie walked in. Maggie could tell she was talking to Caroline in Rosemont. She hoped Hannah would tell her that she was staying on Seaward.

Maggie had showered and dressed and she was brushing her hair, which fell in shiny waves down her back, when she saw Paul through her bedroom window. He was standing on the dock staring at the Cash Floe. Maggie raised the window and shouted a greeting.

She gave the mirror one last glance and bounded down the stairs. "I'm off with Paul," she called to Hannah.

"If Bill finishes at a decent hour, he's coming over for dinner," Hannah shouted back. "I think I'll grill a pork tenderloin."

Maggie waved her approval and focused her attention on Paul, who was waiting by the boat. He had untied the bowline, and Maggie hopped aboard.

"It's a wonderful afternoon for a ride to Edisto," he said.

"I agree. You take her into the Beaufort River. I'll check the chart and keep an eye on the GPS."

The boat glided through two-foot waves, and Maggie settled back to enjoy her afternoon. Paul reached for her hand. She felt a melting sensation somewhere in her chest, but she cautioned her heart to take it slow.

"I think we turn into the waterway very soon," she said. "We want to take the Ashepoo cut. It's quicker than going out to Morgan Reef and into the Atlantic. It's a smoother ride, too."

Side by side, Maggie and Paul watched for the turn, and together they caught sight of a buoy they needed to guide them.

Paul shielded his eyes from the afternoon sun and pointed to the horizon. "Is that a shrimp boat coming our way?"

Maggie squinted in the direction Paul pointed. "It may be a barge going from Charleston to Savannah," she said. She picked up a pair of binoculars and focused on the ship. "That's not a barge!" she exclaimed. "That's the Mary Grace. Quick, make the turn. Then hide behind the bank and let's get a better look at what's going on. Obviously, this is why they're never on schedule. They're not sticking to their route. Looks like they're coming from one of the outer islands, but most of them are uninhabited."

Paul cut the engine, and Maggie watched the Mary Grace slice through the water on the main waterway. The boat was packed with Hispanics, and it was hard to tell if Randy and Dianne were even on board.

"Quick, give me your cell phone," Maggie said. "I haven't replaced mine. I'll call 9-1-1 and tell them to find Bill. Maybe we can get him to meet the ferry at the Beaufort marina. Looks like that's where they're headed." She glanced at her watch. "They've missed their five o'clock landing at Markley."

"Why would hauling a bunch of people require the sheriff?" Paul asked as he handed her the phone.

"I remember Juan made a big point about having a green card. Suppose those people don't and Randy and Dianne are bringing them in illegally?" She tore her eyes from the Mary Grace and looked up at Paul. "Does all this sound crazy?"

"Not to me," Paul answered. He started the Cash Floe and turned her toward Edisto. "The only reason it doesn't make sense is where are the ferry people making money? If aliens are coming here illegally, would they have money to pay for transportation? There may be more people besides the ferry company involved."

Maggie dialed the phone and asked the dispatcher to make sure Bill got the message to meet the Mary Grace, and she explained why it was important. She clicked the phone closed.

"The dispatcher promised to relay the message. I just hope he gets it in time." A thought occurred to her, and she grabbed Paul's arm. "This could be the reason Cotton was killed. He found out who was bringing in illegal workers. It has to be a local. Maybe not on Seaward but in the lowcountry. If I call Hannah, she'll let me know if Bill got my message."

"I'm not taking us back," Paul said firmly. "This is the first outing I've had since I left Lady's Island to hide out and finish my book. Let's let the sheriff and his crew follow up on this."

Maggie didn't argue. She pointed toward the shore. "Look, there's the restaurant. Crowded, too. Crab cake night on Edisto. I'll take her to the dock, and you tie her up."

Maggie and Paul had to wait a while for a table, but she assured him the food would be worth it. When they were finally seated, and Maggie was gazing into her handsome date's eyes, she resolved to put everything but Paul out of her mind. She and Paul chatted about nothing in particular, and Maggie was delighted to learn he had taught English at a private academy on Lady's Island.

"Until my first book hit the best-seller list, I thought I would spend the rest of my life quoting Shakespeare to bored kids in English Lit," he said with an exaggerated shudder.

Maggie was fascinated with his stories about life in an English class, and Paul agreed with her assertions that local crabs were tastier than any that could be shipped in.

The sun was disappearing by the time Paul pointed the Cash Floe back toward Seaward. The ride didn't last long enough for either of them. Maggie rested her head on the back of her seat and closed her eyes, but she opened them just a slit to steal a look at the fascinating man beside her. The wind kept whipping his hair into his eyes, and Maggie made a mental note to buy him the perfect cap for future outings. It was easy to imagine spending more time with Paul, but maybe she was taking too much for granted. He smiled at her just then, and she was suddenly sure that he would want to see her again.

As they approached her dock, Maggie saw Bill, Hannah, and Robert waiting by the water. They all had full wine glasses in their hands.

Hannah raced into the house to check on her roasted green beans while the men tied up the boat. "I'm trying something new," she explained when she walked back to the dock. "Whole fresh green beans drizzled with olive oil and roasted with garlic."

Robert walked to the grill and checked on Hannah's marinated tenderloin.

"Having a late dinner, I see," Maggie commented.

Bill handed Maggie and Paul a glass of red wine. "I had a long day, which translates into a late dinner," he said. "Randy has been arrested. At the moment, he hasn't said anyone else is involved. All we know now is that he's been bringing what he called 'wetbacks' into the country from an island in Georgia. They were brought here by someone posing as a fisherman and guide for Gulf Stream fishing. The feds are working on that end of it. I think someone hired Randy and Dianne to do the dirty work. We'll know more tomorrow."

Bill took a sip of his wine. "I had an idea this was going on. When I got your call I was already at the dock on Goat Island. No one goes over there, and the back end is connected to the mainland when the tide is out. That's why the Mary Grace kept an erratic schedule. They had to drop their illegal passengers when the tide was low. Then the Mexicans would slip into town and either find jobs or move on to other towns. Myrtle Beach has lots of jobs, and they are migrating up the coast." Bill's chest seemed to expand just a little.

150

"Sheriff Hammond is pleased that I figured this one out. I think he'll make me a job offer when he gets back next week."

Hannah's eyes glowed. Maggie wondered if Bill would have known anything about Randy's illegal runs had she not seen the Mary Grace in Morgan Sound. But she kept that question to herself and let him bask in Hannah's adoration.

"Where's Marianna?" Maggie asked Robert. "I thought she would be with you tonight."

Robert was looking equally pleased with himself. "By the time I heard about the Mary Grace, it was too late to get her over. Looks like I'm going to have to start a ferry service if I want Marianna to move to Seaward. For the short term, I've hired a barge from Charleston to make the run. It'll be here in the morning. I got a couple of waiters to post signs letting people know that the ride is free—tomorrow only," he added hastily. "They'll just have to be patient until I can find a decent ferry boat. What do you think about running it from the mainland to Palmetto Bluff instead of Markley Landing? It's not as close to the gated area of the island, but if we offered great coffee…" His eyes opened wide. "It just hit me: Why not a taxi service to the ferry? A small bus or something like that."

Maggie laughed. It was Robert's nature to take a bad situation and turn it into a positive—and lucrative—project. "I've got the Cash Floe, so I won't be using a ferry service, but it sounds great to me," she said.

"Well, time for me to shove off," Paul said. "I'll see you later. I had a wonderful time, Maggie."

"Wait," she said. "I'll walk you to the gate."

Maggie and Paul walked into the kitchen, and he took her hand. Possum popped through the doggie door and looked up adoringly at Maggie.

Paul and Maggie were just about to kiss when they heard a squeal. They pulled away from each other and exchanged startled

151

glances. Maggie jerked open the door. On the back deck, inside a sturdy cardboard box, sat the cutest little pig she had ever seen. He had black spots on a white hide and looked like he weighed about twenty pounds. Maggie picked up the wriggling pig and brought it into the kitchen. Paul took it from her, sat on the floor, and took the piglet into his lap. The pig cuddled against Paul and promptly went to sleep.

Maggie called out the door in a tone that brought Hannah running. She hadn't even taken time to take off her oven mitt.

"How did this pig get here?" Maggie demanded. "Granny said she would keep them."

Hannah waved the oven mitt impatiently. "I have to get the tenderloin off the grill. I thought somebody was dying in here, the way you bellowed!" Maggie just glared and waited for an explanation. "Granny said you could look after this guy until her pen got built. He's your problem for now. I've got to get back to the grill." She stalked away.

"This is blackmail," Maggie fumed. "Granny wants that pen built tomorrow." She looked down at the pig, snoring gently in Paul's lap. "Will he be safe in the back yard, do you think?"

"I'll take him over to my place. Maybe my cat, Sampson, will like this chubby little squealer. He's missed his litter mate since she died last year."

Maggie was touched by the tenderness this big man showed the little creature. "You're an animal lover, too," she said. "Call me in the morning. I'll have Juan at Granny's to start building before the sun comes up. Little pig can move back."

Paul scratched the pig's snout gently and stood up. "We'll see how it goes. Thanks for taking me away from the middle of a stalled chapter."

With the piglet between them, they shared a lingering kiss.

Maggie floated back to her guests. Everyone had filled a plate, and they were deep in conversation about the recent crimes on the island.

Robert wanted to hear about the progress of the murder investigation. He and Maggie agreed that Cotton would not have been a party to what had been going on with the Mary Grace. Bill thought Salty George or one of his friends might be involved, but he had no proof.

"It's out of my hands," he said. "The feds are taking over, and I'm back on the murder."

Maggie heard Possum bark, and she looked up to see Jim Hamilton walk across the yard.

"I came to tell Robert that we closed early," he said. He helped himself to a glass of Chardonnay, sat next to Maggie, and joined the conversation.

"Busy night at the café," he said. "Our special sold out. Sorry you didn't come, Maggie."

Maggie smiled but didn't answer.

"I was just about to tell everyone that we got an I.D. on the woman who drowned," Bill said. "Found her driver's license in a car parked in the marina lot. Had been there for two days." Bill set his plate on the grass next to his chair and kept talking. "Her name was Megan Sanders. She was from Georgetown."

Jim dropped his glass, and it shattered against a cement planter. "Meg Sanders?" he gasped. "I know her. I've worked with her."

Thirteen

Maggie woke to the spatter of raindrops on the window-pane. She couldn't hear any hammering. Apparently, Juan had found her note and had gone to build Granny's pigsty, thank God.

Maggie's clock told her it was 9:25. She loved having her own schedule, not having to commute into a busy city for work. Today, she would spend time on Marianna's house and get ready to present a few new ideas when they met at the end of next week. Hannah had said she would be over at Rose Cottage getting more junk packed away for removal.

Maggie thought back to last evening. It had certainly ended strangely. Jim had explained that Megan Sanders had been an employee at his restaurant in Georgetown. He thought maybe she had come to Beaufort to ask him for a job at the Tabby Café, but she had never contacted him.

When someone mentioned that Megan and Maggie looked a lot alike, Jim had answered that they weren't that similar. He insisted that whoever had pushed Maggie into the river had probably meant it as a joke, and he thought maybe Sherm Pritchard was to blame.

Maggie confessed that the same idea had crossed her mind.

When he was ready to leave, Jim had asked Maggie to walk back to the restaurant with him to take another look at the menu for the wine-tasting and oyster roast, but she had pleaded exhaustion.

Maggie climbed out of bed and padded to the shower, thinking about her plans for the day. At the top of her list was the Shrimp Festival on the mainland. A blessing of the fleet was planned and a wonderful arts and crafts show. The area boasted an abundance of artists and craftsmen. She might find local art for Marianna at the festival. She picked up the phone and dialed the number for Hannah's cell, making a mental note to replace her own cell phone when she went into town.

Maggie couldn't talk Hannah into going with her to the festival. Hannah said she would pull some fabric swatches for Marianna and meet Maggie and Bill at the Red Eye for dinner.

So Maggie would have the whole day to enjoy the festival. She made a list of items she wanted to pick up at the Piggly Wiggly while she was on the mainland, and she took a large canvas bag from the closet. It was easier to haul groceries from the dock in canvas than in flimsy plastic.

Just before she headed out the door, the phone rang.

"I had a great time," Paul said.

"Isn't it fun to make day trips in my boat?" Maggie answered. "How's the pig? Did he sleep all night?"

"Granny might be upset. Sampson thinks Little Pig—that's his name now, you know—is a cat. They spent the night on the bottom of my bed. I think they're bonding."

"If he doesn't bother you, keep him today. I'm going to town. Need anything?"

"You're going in this weather?" Paul didn't sound happy. "Will you be okay?"

"It's not a thunderstorm, just a little rain. I need to practice going alone from my dock to the downtown marina."

"Just be careful," Paul said, and Maggie's heart did a little dance when she heard the warm tone in his voice. "If you have time, could you go by the Beaufort library? My name has come to the top of the list for a new Brandon Childers sci-fi. That's the only genre I'm able to read when I'm in the middle of plotting a mystery."

I'll get to see him today, Maggie thought happily. But when she spoke, she forced herself to sound casual. "I'll drop it by on my way home this afternoon."

155

"Then I'll take you to dinner," Paul said, making Maggie's smile widen.

"Join us at the Red Eye. Bill and Hannah will be there."

Maggie replaced the receiver and hurried to the boat. The rain had let up some, but the wind blew water from the live oaks, and she was soaked before she reached the dock. *Maybe this place should be called Mossy Oaks with all the Spanish moss in the trees*, she thought. Then she rejected the idea. She still liked the sound of "Palmetto Grove."

Even in the rain, the ride was exhilarating, and from her dock to the marina was only a twenty-minute trip. It had taken the Mary Grace more than forty-five.

Moses, who had worked at the marina as long as anyone could remember, helped Maggie tie up the Cash Floe. "Fill 'er up," Maggie instructed. "I'll be back later today to settle up. I'm going to the festival and then a little shopping."

Maggie walked into the parking lot, thinking about her day rather than where she was going. She walked straight into Salty George.

"I thought you might be looking for me," he said. "Just got back from a half-day trawl. Caught two good-sized ones. How's the boat? Guess you know they're gonna let you keep it."

Maggie frowned. "Keep my boat? What do you mean?"

"Guess you didn't hear. Come on in the coffee shop with me. I'll fill you in."

Maggie and Salty George found a small table near the door. Festival crowds pushed into the open doors to get out of the drizzle and gawk at the old house where the owners served cappuccino and local history in equal doses. Maggie enjoyed this place, and she settled in for a talk with Salty George.

He took a sip of black coffee and wiped his beard with a paper napkin. "That no-account cousin who was always telling me he needed money flat out lied."

"You mean the one I bought my boat from? It wasn't used in hauling illegal aliens, was it?"

"He used the Cash Floe for pleasure. He needed a bigger boat to help the Mary Grace offload those poor people. He couldn't keep both. His wife would have wondered where he got all that money." Salty George made an angry, rumbling sound deep in his chest. "I'm still not sure how many people were in on this deal. Glad I didn't see my way clear to go in with him for what he called a fishing boat. Feds said your boat sale was legal and binding, so you got nothing to worry about." Salty George's scowl faded. "I got to go on home," he said. "The wife and I are coming back for the music at the festival tonight. Soggy Bottom Band is playing. That's good dancin' music."

Maggie decided to check out the art show being held in one of the old homes on the square. The Abigail Pinckney Hempleworth house was recognized by the historic association around 1967. Maggie had heard some sad tales about that house. The Federal-style mansion had been built around 1822. Money from indigo trading was probably the source of the Hempleworth fortune.

Maggie studied the house as she ascended the stairs to the front door. At the entrance, she was welcomed by a docent for the museum. At the end of 1974, a foundation for the preservation of old homes in the area had refurbished the house, and the Lowcountry Art Museum used it to display art and antiques. Area schoolchildren made a pilgrimage each year when the small garden in back was in bloom.

Maggie passed through the door and showed her membership card. Stella Barnes stepped in front of her.

"Would you like to see my work?" she asked. "This is my first show. I had hoped that Jim would invite you here today. I've seen you with him a few times, but he never introduced us. I have the original that won a prize at the Royal Inn show a few weeks ago."

So that's why she's here, Maggie thought. Why hadn't Jim ever mentioned Stella?

Maggie followed Stella into a side room. On the far wall hung the perfect painting of palmetto trees, bright green against clear blue water, and a jon boat on the shore. Maggie would hang the painting over the mantle at Palmetto Grove. It seemed she had picked the perfect name for her cottage. This picture confirmed it.

"I want this one," Maggie said. "Will you sell it?"

"I have some wonderful prints that you may be able to use for your Ribaut Inn project. Jim has filled me in on all the news. Maybe we can make a deal. I'll sell you this painting at a discount if you'll consider using some of my prints for your project."

"Actually," Maggie said, "I came to look for the right piece to fit into a new client's home. I haven't seen it yet, but I'll keep looking. I'll give the docent my credit card, and you can wrap up the painting for me."

"I'll have it ready for you this afternoon. I can put it in your car for you."

Maggie shook her head. "I'm traveling by boat today. I have a few more errands before I go back, so I'll send Moses from the dock to pick it up." Maggie was curious about this redhead who kept popping up. She wanted to ask about her relationship with Jim but couldn't figure out how to broach the subject tactfully. She decided to make polite small talk instead.

"Have you tried any food from the participating restaurants?" she asked.

"I'm partial to my husband's cooking," Stella answered. "He's opening this place in Savannah. I'm going there tomorrow to hang some prints. It's a scary proposition, opening a new restaurant. It takes a while to draw in a steady clientele. And the public is fickle. I'm glad Jim has made a name for himself at the Tabby."

Now Maggie was more curious than ever. She paid for the painting and left for the library, but she couldn't stop wondering. Jim must be a friend of Stella's and her husband, who was also a chef, apparently. When Stella was in town, Jim must feel responsible to look after her, Maggie told herself. She tried to think of a way to ask Jim about Stella without being too pushy. She didn't want to seem jealous, though she had to admit she was still attracted to him. Maybe she and Jim could visit the friend's restaurant in Savannah.

The festival's 5K walk and run had finished by the time Maggie picked up Paul's book and the groceries she needed. Sweating participants rounded the tents on the wharf. Under each tent, a restaurant had cooked its best shrimp dish. For a few tickets purchased at the gate, Maggie was able to sample a cup of gumbo soup and several barbecued shrimp on a skewer.

She was wiping barbecue sauce from her lips with a paper napkin when she saw Robert walking her way. "I'm on my way to pick up Marianna at the Inn. I'm trying to talk the feds into selling me the Mary Grace. They've confiscated her, you know. The barge was too breezy this morning, but I think the coffee made up for it. You want to walk over to the Inn with me?"

Maggie shook her head. "I've had enough of city life. I've found the perfect picture for my cottage, and I want to get back before the weather gets worse. We've got a tropical storm off the coast, you know, and it's supposed to dump some rain on us."

Robert gave her a thumbs-up. "Living your life by the weather is a good idea when you travel by boat. Stay safe and dry."

Maggie walked slowly back to the dock. She had eaten a bit too much and was feeling sluggish. Moses was holding a package when she arrived. "Miss Barnes left this for you," he said.

Maggie stowed the painting in the Cash Floe's cabin. She wrapped a blanket around it and pulled the boat away from the shore. It was raining lightly when she pulled into Paul's dock and tooted the horn. He waved from the porch and hurried down the hill to meet her.

"I brought your book," she said. Maggie knew she could have waited until they met at the restaurant to give him the book, but she wanted to see him. She wanted him to see the painting she had bought. Somehow it seemed right for him to be the first person she would share it with.

"Come on up to the house," he said. "Maybe you can tell me how to make it more cheerful. I took the boar's head off the wall, but it still smells like a hunting lodge."

As they climbed the hill, they brainstormed about what they might do to brighten his island home. "Animal prints are popular now," Maggie said. "Maybe we can do something with that. We could make one cheerful room where you work. Since you're renting, it's silly to spend a lot on decorating."

"My lease runs out at the beginning of the year, and the place goes on the market. I've given thought to buying it as a retreat for writing. I've gotten a lot done here. The view is spectacular, inspiring."

Maggie glanced back toward the water. "I understand. I feel that way about my view. Let's hope this side of Seaward is always safe from summer people."

"Oh," Paul said, "before I forget, I need to tell you that Bill called a few minutes ago. Wanted to know if I'd seen you today. Did you pick up a cell phone while you were in town? I'd like to write down the number."

Maggie smacked her palm against her forehead. "I can't believe I forgot again. But I found the perfect painting for my cottage. A watercolor of palmetto trees with a river like Lawson Creek in the background. I got so excited about it, I forgot to check on the phone. That is on the top of my list for my next trip to town. I did remember to grocery shop," Maggie added with a chuckle. "Hannah requires a lot of diet soda."

Paul held open the back door of his home. "Come in and meet Sampson. He's a fierce Siamese—without claws. When he lets out his mournful yowl, the house shakes, so don't let him scare you."

Maggie stepped back into the nineteenth century when she entered the lodge. The living room was huge, with a kitchen tacked on at the back. The walls and furniture were dark and depressing. She ran her hands over a wall. It looked like pine, but it had a musty cypress smell.

"If you buy this place, get someone to clean this wood," she said. "Lots of cigarettes and even more cigars have been smoked in here. A thorough cleaning job would make it shine, though. It could be really pretty."

Paul nodded. "When Juan comes to build my bookcases, I'll ask if he or someone he knows would like to take on the job. You've inspired me to brighten this place up a little." He snapped his fingers. "I just figured out what I'm going to do about my hero's love life." He gave her an appreciative smile. "You might just turn out to be my muse, Maggie."

Maggie ducked her head so he wouldn't see her blush. "I'll leave you to your writing then," she said. "I'm going to check on the progress of our big party at the Tabby."

"I'll see you at the Red Eye tonight." He pulled Maggie to him and kissed her, gently at first and then more passionately.

She stumbled down the hill to the boat. She could still feel his lips on hers and his strong arms around her. She had forgotten to show him her new painting, but there'd be plenty of opportunities, she knew now.

By the time Maggie arrived back at Palmetto Grove, the rain had turned into a downpour, and a fierce wind blew. Maggie ran for the cottage without the painting. Juan and Hannah, seated on a covered portion of the deck sipping diet colas, watched her struggle across the yard.

Maggie plopped down on a chair to catch her breath.

"Got rained out at Rose Cottage," Hannah said. "Maybe this'll pass before long. The weather report in the paper said the tropical storm wouldn't hit this area too hard. Sure hope Sherm was right, for once. Juan's almost finished the sleeping porch," she added, and Juan nodded confirmation. "Bet you'll be sleeping out in the fresh air by tomorrow night." Hannah sipped her cola and rocked contentedly for a minute. "Oh, Marianna called. She wants to buy the Mayflower chair at the art show. She actually said it must have come over on its namesake."

"She's talking about the chair the docent sits in at the front door? I'll bet she doesn't know the story."

"Neither do I," Hannah said.

Juan, sitting between Hannah and Maggie, turned to watch each woman as she talked and struggled to keep up with their rapid-fire conversation. It was like trying to keep up with a volleyball game, he decided, and he gave up and sat back in his chair.

"The leader of the historical society—I can't remember his name—told me that around 1930, one of the members of the society went to Boston," Maggie told Hannah. "He came back and proclaimed he had an original Mayflower chair. No one bothered to have it authenticated, and it was put in a place of honor at the Hempleworth house. The member who brought back the chair was named Harcourt, I think. He was a young man when he brought it to Beaufort, and when he was old, he was still a hero to the society. He was asked to speak at one of their Founding Fathers meetings. It had been a hot day, and several members decided to spike the lemonade with a batch of homebrew. Mr. Harcourt imbibed more than his share and staggered to the podium for his speech.

"He announced that he had a confession to make. He proceeded to inform the society that, as a young man, he was in the habit of going to the Mayflower Hotel in Boston with some friends. One night, they stole a chair from the hotel and brought it back to Beaufort. They concocted the story about the Mayflower ship, but the only Mayflower it was actually associated with was the hotel. The old man cracked up, but none of the other members thought it was funny in the least." Maggie paused for a second before delivering the punch line. "I think that is why most Harcourts live in the upstate now."

Hannah threw back her head and laughed until her eyes watered. Juan smiled politely. Maggie could tell he had gotten lost long before she finished her story.

"When I share this with Marianna," Maggie said straight-faced, "she may not want to purchase a reproduction of a French Bergere upholstered armchair. It would look funny in a beach house. Although I guess we could cover it in chintz and hide it in her bedroom."

Hannah burst into laughter again. Juan stared at her, looking puzzled.

"Oh, look," Maggie said. "The rain's stopped. I want to see what you've done at Rose Cottage. Then I'll get my painting, and we'll hang it before we meet everyone at the Red Eye. Come on, Juan. Come with us."

Juan stood but he didn't move to follow them. "I want to finish your porch today. Help you move in tomorrow. Have Miss Hannah show you the spot for her outdoor garden room. I will build it for her this winter. She will plant roses and train vines through the slats of the shelter."

"Clematis," Hannah corrected him. "We'll train clematis through the slats. With warm weather eight or nine months of the year down here, it would be silly not to have several outdoor rooms for the cottage. Juan has some friends who'll help us build a deck on the back. That will be our jumping off point. It's calming for me to sit in a garden on a comfortable bench, even in a gentle rain. Maybe we could put a tin roof over one of the spots and grow shady plants. Will hosta grow in the heat down here?"

"I have plenty on the side of my cottage by the live oaks. I also added some Indian hawthorn, and I still want to try hydrangeas. Maybe we can plant those next spring," Maggie said.

Maggie and Hannah walked toward Hannah's new home talking excitedly about their gardening plans. They walked in through the back door, and Maggie could see that most of the clutter had been carted away.

"I can see my grandmother's sideboard in that corner," Hannah said, waving toward an empty wall. "This will be my retreat for security when the outside world is going crazy. I want all the things I love here. My 1940s chair that looks more like sculpture than a piece of furniture." Hannah stopped her breathless plans abruptly and turned to Maggie. "This is all happening pretty fast. Is it okay with you?"

Maggie gave her friend a hug. "I'd hoped you'd like it here. We make great business partners." Maggie hesitated, then decided to say what was on her mind. "I do think you should slow it down with Bill a little, though, play the field. We don't know much about him. You know, it occurs to me that he could even be involved in some of the things that have been happening around here lately."

Hannah's eyes blazed. "Absurd," she snapped. "He wants to take me to Raleigh in a few weeks to meet his sister. I do wish he would find Cotton's killer so all this suspicion and fear would go away. I admit I'm a little nervous about living by myself just now. But Bill feels sure it had to be a snowbird who's left the area." Hannah turned to Maggie for reassurance. "What do you think? You think the killer is gone?"

Maggie thought carefully about her reply. "I think it's time for us to go get my new painting and hang it," she said cheerfully. "Did I tell you it was painted by our redheaded mystery lady, Stella Barnes?"

"The woman that Jim has been seeing?"

"They're friends. Apparently, she's married to a chef named Barnes in Savannah."

Hannah digested this new information for a moment. "Interesting. I don't think Bill knows that." Then she waggled her eyebrows at Maggie. "So he's not romantically involved with the redhead. That puts Jim back in the ballgame, doesn't it? I thought I'd be the one playing the field, choosing among the men of Seaward. So who's it gonna be? Jim or Paul?"

Maggie walked out the door without answering. She kept quiet during the walk back to Palmetto Grove while Hannah talked endlessly about her plans.

When they reached the cottage, Maggie took Possum down by the water and turned her loose. Possum immediately plunged in. She loved an afternoon swim, and when the tide was high, she didn't get plough mud stuck in her coat.

While Possum was frolicking, Maggie stepped onto the Cash Floe to retrieve her painting. The blanket she had wrapped it in had been thrown in a heap on the deck. The painting was gone. Juan must have taken it to hang over the mantle, she decided. Maggie hoped he knew the proper height over the mantle, or maybe he had just propped it there until she came to give him instructions.

Just then, she saw Juan walk onto the porch. "Did you hang the picture already?" she asked. "I hope you didn't yet. I want to take some measurements first."

Juan looked at her blankly. "I have been working on the porch," he said. "I do not know what you mean."

Hannah tossed a stick into the water and laughed as Possum swam to retrieve it. She walked to the porch, humming. "Do you want me to help you bring the picture up to the house from the boat?" she asked.

"It's not in the boat, and it's not in the house," Maggie said angrily. "Call Bill. My Palmetto Grove painting has been stolen."

Fourteen

Bill strode across the Cash Floe's deck and declared dramatically that the picture had indeed been stolen. Maggie crossed her arms and gave him her "I'll hang you higher than a curtain" look, but she resisted telling him that he was stating the obvious. Juan and Hannah stood near the dock and watched the tide ebb. They thought it wise to keep their distance just now.

"I can't understand how this happened," Maggie said. "Moses put the picture on the boat, and I stowed it away. I stopped at Paul's for a few minutes. I don't remember seeing it when I got back in the boat. It had started raining again, and I wanted to get here quickly. The only other time it could have been taken was when we were at Rose Cottage. If somebody had been creeping around, Possum would have had a fit."

"Maybe she knew the person," Bill argued. "Possum doesn't bark at friends, does she?"

"Why would a friend steal my picture?" Maggie thundered. "For that matter why would anyone want a picture of a palmetto grove with a bateau?" She flopped onto a seat on the deck, and the rain-soaked cushion squished beneath her, but she hardly noticed.

From the edge of the water, Juan shouted, causing everyone to jump. "Look, Miss Maggie. Look what is next to your boat."

Bill looked over the side of the boat to where Juan was pointing. "It's bubble wrap," he said, "and it's evidence." He jumped over the side and sank up to his shins in gray plough mud. He tried to take a step and discovered he was stuck. "Help me!" he yelled.

Hannah shrieked and jumped into the mud to help, but she was instantly trapped in the ooze up to her knees. On her first step, her shoe had come off, and she cut her foot on a bed of oyster shells.

"Help us," she pleaded. "We've fallen into quicksand. Throw us a life preserver from the boat. We're going down."

Maggie stared down from her perch at the two of them struggling to get free. She knew it would be impossible to walk out to get them. That wasn't quicksand, but plough mud could suck a person up to the neck and hold them like dried cement. Maybe she could throw them a lifeline. Juan ran to the house. Maggie shouted at him to come back, then realized what he must be up to. She climbed off the boat and followed him. In the meantime, Hannah and Bill were yelling louder than the rails in the reeds. The more they twisted and struggled, the deeper they sank. Mud had spattered their faces and their clothes. But Bill held tightly to the bubble wrap.

"Just be still," Maggie yelled. "We're coming for you. Juan is going to put planks down in the mud and step out to get you."

Juan placed the planks carefully, making sure he didn't tumble in and become victim number three.

"The painting is in this bubble wrap, or at least there's something in here that feels like a painting." Bill shouted. "Shove the boards this way, and I'll hand it to you. Then get Hannah."

Hannah's hair had turned a marshy gray, and she had started to cry. Juan handed the painting to Maggie, then grabbed Hannah by the waist and pulled her onto the boards. With Juan's help, she limped to a chair in the yard and collapsed.

"This better be the best painting I've ever seen," she growled. She swiped some mud from her feet, trying to judge how badly they were bruised and cut.

In a matter of minutes, Bill was free as well, and he rushed to Hannah to comfort her, which caused her to start crying again. "It's all right now," he said, holding her to him protectively. "You're safe now."

Maggie rolled her eyes but kept her mouth shut.

Bill wasted no time taking charge again. "Let's clean up and get this bubble wrap to the lab." He helped Hannah to her feet.

"Sorry you two had to experience the lowcountry baptism," Maggie said. "Almost everyone who goes after oysters the first time gets stuck. There's no way to get out gracefully. At least you didn't have to wait for the tide to come back to the dock. That would have been six hours in the mud. Hope you still want to eat oysters after this."

"Yeah, but I think I'll let someone else gather them for us," Bill said with a hint of a grin. "We've got the painting, and that's what we wanted."

"I can't imagine why anyone would dump it overboard—unless they were looking for something else," Maggie said. "I'll put gloves on to unwrap it, Bill. Then at least you won't have more prints to trace. Let's get you two cleaned up." Maggie gave Juan a pat on the back. "You're the greatest."

Juan beamed and ducked his head. He followed Maggie into the house.

Hannah and Bill left a trail of mud across the kitchen floor, but Maggie didn't complain. She ran a damp mop over the floor and had cleaned up the mess by the time Bill came down, freshly showered. Maggie had managed to scare up some work-out clothes that were big enough for him, if not particularly masculine in cut and color. Hannah called down the stairs that it might take her a few days to get clean again, and she added that no one was to disturb her for a while.

Maggie propped her painting, miraculously undamaged, on the mantle. She and Bill studied it carefully, both trying to figure out why anyone would want to steal it.

Finally, Bill shrugged. "A regular painting," he said. "It looks like all the palmetto trees in your yard. The jon boat looks a little out of place, though."

"There aren't any numbers on it. It looks like the artist started to paint the numbers, then smeared them. I wonder if Stella painted this from memory or from a real picture. The boat is tilted, almost on its side, like it was swaying or rocking in the breeze. Very realistic. Guess you'll ask her."

"You can bet on it," Bill answered. "I plan to track her down tomorrow. Got one of the deputies coming over in our boat to take the wrap to the lab. That's about all we can do tonight. I'm going to meet him at the dock near the Tabby. I'll see you and Hannah at the Red Eye."

Maggie walked slowly up the stairs to the bedroom. None of this made any sense. This painting certainly wasn't valuable enough to steal. A thief would only steal it if he were trying to hide something. She undressed in her bedroom and stepped into the shower. She turned on the water full blast and stuck her head under the stream, trying to wash away troubling thoughts. She pulled on a pair of denim Capri pants with her favorite white V-neck sweater.

Hannah was waiting for Maggie in the living room. She had scrubbed her face until it glowed. She was staring at the mantle. "This was worth a trip through the mud. She's a good artist."

"She wants us to use some of her prints in the Ribaut Inn project. Think we might get Chandler to cough up the money for real paintings?"

"Let's work on that idea. The colors of her salty marsh look like she lifted them from the mud and put them on the canvas. Realistic. And haunting. I love her work."

Juan was feeding Possum when the two women left for the Red Eye. He waved and smiled.

"I need to talk to Jim before I meet you at the Red Eye," Maggie told Hannah. "Order a Pinot Noir for me. Jim wants to do some last minute changes to our menu for the wine-tasting and oyster roast. Tell Paul I'm on my way."

Maggie veered off the path and took a shortcut to the Tabby. She didn't go this way often because there were lots of Virginia creeper and poison oak on the path, and she was allergic. It made her itch to think about it.

She was stepping carefully over weeds and brush when she heard voices. It sounded like a man and a woman. Then she heard the man yell. Neither voice sounded familiar.

She tiptoed closer. She caught a glimpse of a man—well, probably it was a man—in a black T-shirt as he ran through the woods. He was headed in the direction Maggie had just come.

Maggie listened as he crashed through the brush, then she shrugged and turned back toward the Tabby Café.

When she got to the back door, she could hear bits of conversations and dishes clattering from the dining room. She didn't see anyone in the kitchen. Jim stepped out of the darkness at the side of the café and greeted Maggie with a warm smile. "I'm glad you came," he said. "Want to have some dinner? I've got a great special tonight."

Maggie averted her eyes. "Thanks, but I'm meeting Hannah at the Red Eye. I just wanted to ask what changes you've made for the party. The weather is perfect for an oyster roast."

"I got the ale company to supply beer. May be too late now, but I was thinking we could make a couple of salads. We may have some vegetarians in the bunch. Okay with you?"

"If Robert thinks we need it," Maggie answered. "I'll come over early in the morning and help you get organized. Do you know if the Civil War nuts are still around? Thought I saw one running through the woods."

"Oh, they'll probably be here a while," Jim said with a smirk. "Good excuse for them to get away from the wives, since most of them don't play golf. If you hear cannon fire tonight, don't get out of bed. They're probably shooting each other."

171

He looked down at her with an expression Maggie couldn't interpret. She thought maybe he had heard about her outings with Paul, and she felt a twinge of guilt. But she still wasn't sure where he stood with Stella, and she meant to find out. "After the party tomorrow night, I want you to come see the painting I bought from your friend Stella. It's perfect for my mantle. There's a funny story behind it."

A young man Maggie recognized as a waiter stuck his head out the back door. "Chef, we need you," he said.

Maggie squeezed Jim's hand briefly. "I'll tell you about it tomorrow night," she promised.

As she walked toward the Red Eye, she thought over Jim's reaction to the mention of Stella's name—or the lack of reaction, to be more precise. Surely, they were just friends. He hadn't made any effort to keep the women from knowing about each other, but he hadn't introduced them, either.

Paul stepped onto the path in front of her. "I've been waiting for you. You certainly seem preoccupied," he said. "Do I need to pay you for your thoughts?"

His cashmere sweater fit perfectly over a black turtleneck and brought out the golden flecks in his eyes. He took Maggie's arm as they walked.

She looked again at Paul's turtleneck and thought about the man she had seen running through the woods. "Did you see anyone in the woods as you walked this way?" she asked.

"A bunch of Civil War re-enactors are trying to get their cannon through the muddy path and out to their campsite. I watched them for a few minutes."

Maggie rolled her eyes. "I can't imagine why these people would want to play in the mud and not even have a decent meal." She dismissed the re-enactors with a shake of her head. "I hope Little Lavender has cooked something special for us."

172

Maggie and Paul joined Hannah, Bill, Robert, and Marianna at the end of a long table in the middle of the room. Dickie and his cousin Jefferson were throwing darts at the other end of the pub. Sallie Jo had taken the pink plastic curlers out of her hair and stood behind the bar. Her face was pudgy and bright, and she wore a green tent dress she had made herself to accommodate her swollen belly. She caught sight of Maggie and waved her over.

"Granny and Althea have the pig issue settled," she declared, "in case you haven't heard. Juan has them penned in, and Granny is as happy as a pig in ... Oops, there's the phone. Prob'ly a takeout order." She waddled away.

By the time Maggie took her seat beside Paul, a waiter had appeared. "What's the special?" she asked.

"Shrimp and grits," he said. "We've added extra Tabasco to ours, so if you like it spicy, you're in luck. It's got sherry in it, too. Don't need nothing else with it if you order the small salad. It'll make you feel like you got beach sand in your blood."

"Sounds great to me. How about you, Paul?"

"Same for me," Paul answered. "Does the rest of the table agree?"

Robert and Marianna took their eyes off each other long enough to look up and nod, and Hannah and Bill made it unanimous.

Paul squeezed Maggie's hand under the table. "I'm going to walk out to the front of the building for a minute. I've been trying to call my agent. I'll be back before dinner comes."

Maggie watched Paul walk away. She caught herself ogling his backside, and she felt her face go red. She turned her attention to the people at the table, hoping they hadn't noticed.

"I think a home drying center sounds like a wonderful idea," Marianna was saying to Hannah. "It would be such a bother to take clothes to the mainland to be cleaned. You sure this isn't something you've made up?"

173

Hannah held her hand up as if she were taking an oath in court. "I'll take you to the Charleston Home Center next week, show you what one looks like. You can dry sweaters flat, tumble towels, and hang dresses all with the same dryer. The upper cabinet removes odors and nothing shrinks."

"Sounds like I want one too," Maggie chimed in.

"Bill told us what happened with your painting today, Maggie," Robert said. "Glad you got it back. I can't wait to see it over your mantle."

"Well, I'll tell you what," Maggie answered. "After dinner let's order takeout dessert and go back to Palmetto Grove. You'll all love that painting. Marianna, you may want to take a look at some of Stella's work. Hannah and I are going to show some of her paintings to your brother. They would be perfect for the Inn."

Paul slid back into his seat next to Maggie and gave her hand another squeeze, but he looked a little grumpy.

"My agent seems to think I can sign books all the time," he complained. "I came over from Lady's Island to write. I told him I'll be happy to sign after the Christmas rush. I don't think I'll be answering my phone for at least a week." He smiled at Maggie and added, "Unless you plan to call."

Before long, the topic turned once more to the island murder.

"I'm tired of telling people I have no new leads," Bill said. "Some of the evidence seemed to point to what was going on with the Mary Grace, but that didn't pan out. We've questioned everyone, run down every lead. There is nothing that points to a primary suspect. Dianne and Randy were taking orders from their ringleader—Salty George's relative, as it turns out. But nothing ties him to Cotton's murder. And we still don't know what happened with that Georgetown woman, if she drowned accidentally or if she was murdered. I'm beginning to think that a snowbird killed Cotton and moved on."

The mood around the table was turning gloomy, and Maggie didn't want the evening to be spoiled. "Let's take a Mississippi mud pie home. I'll make a pot of Columbian decaf, and we can sit around the living room and christen the Palmetto Grove."

The night was cool enough to turn their breath into puffs of fog when they stepped out of the restaurant. Paul put his arm around Maggie as they walked with the group to her cottage. Maggie carried the pie carefully with both hands. Everybody was in a cheerful mood, and she felt a deep contentment. This was how she had hoped life on Seaward would be, full of good friends, good food, and beautiful scenery with lots of peace and quiet.

Just then the Civil War cannon boomed in the distance. "So much for peace and quiet," she grumbled to herself.

"Did you leave the gate open?" Bill asked as they approached the house.

"Maybe Juan accidentally left it ajar," Maggie answered.

Maggie led the way into the cottage. When they all had trooped into the dark living room, Maggie flipped the lights on with a flourish. "Ta-da!" she sang.

Her friends made no comment at all, and then Maggie saw why. She let out an indignant yell, stomped toward the mantle, lost her footing, and fell. The pie hit the floor first, and when she followed, her face smashed right into the middle of it. She came up covered in chocolate and whipped cream and graham crackers. A pecan was stuck squarely in the middle of her forehead.

"My picture has been stolen—again!" she wailed.

Fifteen

Sunshine streamed through Maggie's living room windows. The tropical storm had moved up the coast to New England, leaving behind a glorious day for the oyster roast. The temperature gauge on the porch hovered between sixty-five and sixty-six degrees—cool and clear for Robert's first foray into big-time entertainment at the Tabby Café.

Maggie had finished the notes for Marianna's beach house. She and Hannah would go over them tomorrow. She stared morosely at the empty space above the mantle. Bill hadn't made any progress on finding the painting. None of the prints from the bubble wrap were on file with the FBI or the State Law Enforcement Division.

Maggie walked out the back door, making sure not to let it slam. Hannah was still asleep. Juan had left earlier to start building the shelves at Paul's lodge. He had promised to come back later to help carry furniture to the new sleeping porch.

Before Maggie reached her gate, she remembered that the outdoor cover for the daybed had not arrived. She had stashed several pieces of canvas in the bottom of the kitchen broom closet. "I'll use that for now," she said to Possum. She lugged it from behind the broom and vacuum cleaner.

And then she saw something that made her doubt her own eyes.

"I don't believe it!" she cried. Her voice was loud enough to wake Hannah, who came barreling down the steps two at a time.

Maggie sat on the floor with her legs crossed in the lotus position, but she wasn't calm. On her lap lay the Palmetto Grove painting. She looked up at Hannah. "Someone is trying to make me crazy," she declared solemnly.

"It's almost as if someone stole it to check it for something or to examine it, and then gave it back," Hannah said. "Look at every inch of it."

Both women stared at the picture. The boat numbers were not readable. "I can't remember if the register numbers were clear," Maggie said, scratching her head. "Call Bill, and when he gets in touch with Stella, have him ask her. I'm already late to help Robert and Jim."

Maggie placed the painting in its place of honor over the mantle and headed out the back door. She knew that Hannah would report the newest twist in the theft of the painting to Bill, but she decided to call Stella when she got to Robert's. She had a few questions of her own she wanted to ask.

Laughter and lively music led Maggie up the path and over to the Tabby Café.

The oyster tables were in place by an open fire pit. Jim and Robert huddled over the pit, fiddling with the grill.

"We put the oysters in the sacks over the fire and wet them. Steamed to perfection," Jim said. "Little Lavender has promised to man the grill tonight. Glad you're here, Maggie. Got plenty for you to do. Come in the kitchen. You want to taste the latest sauce?"

Maggie held up her index finger to let Jim know she needed just a minute. "I need to make a phone call. Then I'll meet you in the kitchen."

She walked into Robert's office. The museum number was in his Rolodex. While she waited, she made a mental note to pick up her new cell phone. Stella answered on the third ring.

After a few pleasantries, Maggie got around to what was really on her mind. "Did you paint that picture I bought using a photograph or did you use a real place?"

"Funny you should ask," Stella said. "I just stumbled on that scene one day and knew it was perfect. On a walk around Seaward, I found the boat pulled across a log and almost in a gator creek over by the Tabby Café."

"I know exactly where you mean. Please, could you come and visit me? I want you to see where I hung the painting. It's perfect."

"I'm coming to the party tonight. Maybe I can stop at your place. Jim tells me it's fabulous."

"See you tonight." Maggie hung up wondering if Stella was coming as Jim's date. Or were they friends? Was she married to a guy named Barnes? No time to think about that now.

She walked outside and over to Robert, who was unpacking wine bottles. "I need to check on a few things," she said. "Be back shortly. "She intended to find the bateau before anyone else knew about it.

"Sherman Pritchard is looking for you," Robert told her. "I think he's trying to get another angle on Cotton's death. Murder sells newspapers; that's for sure. He may be looking for a human-interest angle—you know, a feature on the people who knew and loved poor Cotton. Sherm keeps asking me about my plans for the ferry service, too. Pesky little fellow. Oh, and Paul said to tell you he and Juan will be over to help get your porch together this afternoon."

Maggie smiled at the mention of Paul's name, but Robert took no notice. His mind was on the party, not on Maggie's romances. "Boatload of people coming from the mainland. Jim's gone over to the Red Eye. Help him bring the platters back when you have a chance."

Robert went back to the wine bottles, and Maggie headed into the woods. Her legs were beginning to itch. *Should have used bug spray,* she thought. The path was unmarked this way and seldom used. The quiet of the interior reminded her of how each part of the island had its own flavor. Fanning her hands back and forth to keep the gnats and no-see-ums out of her face, she remembered this was called the lowcountry wave. People from other parts of the world thought residents here were being friendly, only to find out the wave kept the bugs out of their mouths.

The walk took longer than she anticipated. The lagoon, she knew, was close to the old Liberty Oak. The ancient and majestic tree used to be the site of many an oyster roast before Robert took over the marina and built the café. She saw the jon boat in the distance and hurried her steps. This was a spawning area for gators, and they were spotted here every spring. She didn't expect to see one at this time of year, but it never hurt to be wary. This island was lovely, but it could be dangerous, too.

She stopped and caught her breath. The vista in front of her was as pretty as the Palmetto Grove painting. Stella had done an excellent job of capturing the lowcountry's wild beauty.

Maggie suddenly caught a familiar scent on the air: stargazer lilies. She walked closer to the boat and found, on the seat next to a worn paddle, a clear vase filled with lilies. Bizarre, she thought. Was this some weird kind of shrine? Could it be for Cotton? Could the killer have used this boat to haul Cotton down to the pier at the café? The inside of the boat seemed spotless, but Maggie wanted to inspect it closely for traces of blood. She knelt at the side of the boat. Red paint had been smeared across the identification numbers, making them impossible to read. Perhaps Bill or the state forensic lab would know how to decipher them.

A sudden breeze stirred nearby palm fronds, and the hollow, scratching sound they made sent a shiver up her spine.

"Better get back before anyone misses me," she said aloud.

Just as she started to rise, something hard slammed against her head. She caught a glimpse of a tree limb as it swung toward her a second time.

Everything went dark, but she caught another whiff of stargazer lilies. Then she slumped, unconscious, against the boat.

Sixteen

Maggie thought she must have been out for hours. Her head throbbed and her limbs were stiff. She itched all over from bug bites. But then she noticed that the sun had only moved a little to the west while she was unconscious. She tried to sit up, but that made her head spin and she feared she would pass out again. It took several minutes for her to struggle into a sitting position, and another ten minutes or so before she felt it was safe to stand.

The boat had disappeared.

She touched the back of her head gently and found a respectable goose egg rising. But she didn't think she had suffered serious damage. It could have been much worse. Whoever attacked her could have killed her had they swung that limb in earnest.

She stumbled through the woods and up to the back of the Tabby. The pain in her head had eased to a dull ache, and the dizziness was all but gone.

"Where have you been?" Jim called. "I brought all the platters and put them in the kitchen. I need help stringing lights by the dock. Robert's down there looking for you. I hope you plan to change clothes. It looks like you've been rolling in mud."

"I had a slight accident," she said. When she saw a look of concern cross his face, she added quickly, "I'm okay, though. I fell as I was running to help you at the Red Eye and bumped my head on something. I'll check in with Robert, change clothes, and see you later."

Maggie walked slowly down toward the dock. Robert was shouting at some harried-looking waiters. Maggie could tell that Robert was uptight about his first party. Most of the proceeds would go to the Seaward Island Children's Fund; a failure wouldn't hurt his wallet, but it would certainly dent his philanthropic intentions.

"Robert, if you have everything under control, I'm going to change clothes and be back to set up the food before the party starts."

He didn't even look her way. "Got reservations for fifty-eight people. Got enough food and drinks for more than that." He waved in her general direction. "See you later." Then he started shouting directions at his workers again.

By the time she got home, Maggie's head was beginning to pound again. She patted Possum and limped into the cottage. She listened for a second and was relieved to find that she was alone in the house. Hannah must have gone to Rose Cottage. There was a note on the table. "Called Bill," Hannah had written. "Stella has a picture of the boat, and there are numbers on it. Bill has gone to the mainland to get the photo and check the registration of the boat. Will be over for the party tonight. I'm having lunch with Sallie Jo to talk about the shower we're giving her."

Good ol' Hannah always took up the slack when they worked together in Rosemont, and she was doing it again. It was a blessing to have her here.

Maggie slowly climbed the stairs to her bedroom, intending to soak in the bathtub. Then she would coat her legs with lotion to stop the itch. Tonight after the party, she would sleep on her porch. The night breezes would bring a welcome chill to the air. Maggie imagined snuggling under her warm duvet cover.

By the time she climbed out of the tub and put on jeans and a black turtleneck under her red cashmere pullover, she heard Juan and Paul banging around downstairs. When she arrived at the screened-in sleeping porch, they had started moving furniture. Juan knew exactly how to place the daybed, and she and Paul put up a hammock in the opposite comer.

181

"I could sleep on this woven hammock," he said with a suggestive grin. She didn't return his smile, though, and he looked away, seeming a little bit hurt. She didn't want to believe he would attack her, but wasn't he always popping up when she was walking around the island? Hadn't he appeared suddenly in her path in the woods the night her painting was stolen from the mantle? She eyed him with suspicion.

"I had a real scare this morning," she said, watching his face intently to judge his reaction. "I got hit on the head and knocked out. I found the boat in my mantle picture."

Paul and Juan stared at her with open mouths. They both looked truly shaken.

"Well, that settles it," Paul said firmly. "You're not going to go to that party tonight if someone has already made an attempt on your life. Has Bill taken your statement?" He touched her cheek gently. "Maybe we should take you to a doctor."

Maggie shook her head. "Bill's on the mainland, and I don't need a doctor. Whoever hit me didn't intend to kill me or do me any real damage. They just didn't want me to examine the boat. I'll be perfectly safe at the party."

Still, she was touched by their concern, which seemed genuine. She had feared they might laugh it off and accuse her of exaggerating or imagining the incident altogether. Or, worse, that she would see a flicker of guilt in Paul's eyes.

Hannah came bouncing in, but she stopped abruptly when she sensed the tension. "Someone attacked Maggie," Paul told her. Hannah's initial reaction was horror and panic, but Maggie downplayed the incident and managed to calm her friend down.

Maggie had a plan, but she had no idea now who she could trust, so she kept it to herself. She would tell everyone she knew that she had seen the boat numbers under the paint, Bill was tracking down the boat's registration, and it was just a matter of time until the killer was caught. She would make sure Sherm got the scoop for the *Times*. That way, her attacker would have no reason to target her again.

The four of them set out for the party. Maggie noted that Paul didn't take her arm, but he stayed very close to her side. She had no idea if his intent was to stalk her or protect her.

The entire population of the lowcountry, it seemed, had come out for Robert's oyster roast. Hannah took off on her own, and a few minutes later, Maggie spotted Jim in the crowd and waved. He rushed over, looking panicked.

"I'm not letting you get hurt again," he said with a mixture of gruffness and tenderness. "Hannah told me what happened to you. Don't wander off by yourself tonight. I have to go get more oyster sauce. While I'm gone, you stay beside Paul or Hannah."

"Bill has the numbers off the killer's boat," she said loudly enough for anyone nearby to hear. "It's the same boat Stella painted in the Palmetto Grove picture. Is she coming tonight?"

Jim shrugged indifferently. "I don't know," he said. "I told her that you and I were going to enjoy oysters together." He put a protective arm around her shoulder. "Nothing will happen to you while your friends are around. Just stay close to one of us, you hear?"

Maggie watched him walk away, then wandered into the crowd. The band cranked up at nine. Sail boaters from as far away as Ocean City, Maryland, partied with the locals.

Althea had come for a visit with Granny, who apparently had taken full advantage of the free beer. The old lady proclaimed proudly to Maggie and anyone else who came near that she was training Little Pig to walk on a leash. To prove her point, she nodded proudly at the piglet at her feet. Indeed, the little fellow seemed perfectly content at the end of a frayed clothesline Granny had turned into a makeshift restraint.

"I got somethin' to share with you, Miss Maggie," Althea said when Granny quieted down. "About Cotton. He left a will with Lefty Jacobs, the fella who does wills for free. Mr. Jacobs says you got money from Cotton in his will, but he don't know where the money is at. I knew Cotton would be good to you. You got him lots of jobs." Althea took Maggie's hand. "You look like you seen a ghost. Are you all right?"

"All this noise is giving me a headache, that's all," Maggie answered.

"I used the money Cotton gave me to buy a shop in Port Royal, did you hear? It's not even really open yet, and people are already comin' to buy. I hope I can work with you and Miss Hannah on some of your projects."

Althea moved away to take her place in line at the shucking table.

At least Maggie knew now where the money had come from and what it was for. Cotton had given half from the sale of his trailer to Althea and the other half to Maggie. Did Delores, his ex-wife, know? Was she trying to get her hands on the money? She was supposed to be long gone, but she could have come back. But how did the woman who drowned in the Beaufort River fit into the equation? Or was her death just a tragic accident?

Paul, who had stayed just a step or two away while Maggie walked through the crowd, suddenly gripped her shoulder. Maggie had forgotten all about him, and she gasped when he touched her.

"You seem to always be lost in thought lately," he said. "What's on your mind?" When she didn't answer, he added, "We aren't going to let you even go inside the restaurant by yourself tonight. Would you care to join me for some wine samples in the main dining room? This is a great party. Let's just relax and have some fun."

He guided her into the dining room, where they came face to face with Sherman Pritchard. He was sipping a California merlot and scanning the crowd. He didn't have his camera bag slung over

184

his shoulder tonight. He must have decided to enjoy the party and let his reporters handle the work, Maggie decided.

"This is a 2002 year from the finest grape-growing region," Sherm told her. Maggie found him pompous and annoying, but she kept these thoughts to herself. Sherm was part of her plan, and she didn't want to make him mad.

"I have a news tip for you," she said. "It's about..."

Sherm held up his hand. "I'm not on duty tonight." He swirled the opaque red liquid in his glass and continued to pontificate. "This has an elegant creaminess and rich fruit flavors. Here, I'll pour you a glass."

Maggie had to force herself to answer civilly. "Not yet. I want to see what the offerings are before I decide what to taste. Look, Paul, there's Salty George and his wife. Let's say hello."

They left Sherm sloshing his wine and explaining its nuances to an unfortunate soul who happened to be standing next to him.

Salty introduced his wife and asked Maggie if she was enjoying her new boat.

At the mention of the Cash Floe, Maggie beamed. "It's perfect for me. I've already taken it to Beaufort and a picnic on Sandibar Island."

Salty George's eyes lit up with a mischievous twinkle. "I heard about that. The rescue guys appreciated the donation. They picked up Scotty's cousin, you know. He's dealing with the feds now." Salty took his wife in his arms and playfully danced her in a circle. "We're going to go cut a rug."

Maggie strolled over to the wine table, and Paul followed. Chandler, Marianna, and Robert were already there, debating the best vintages.

"Great party, isn't it?" Chandler boomed at Maggie. He took a hard look at Paul. "Don't I know you?" Before Paul could answer, Chandler's eyes widened and he shook his finger just under Paul's nose. "You're the one that wrote that bestseller." Paul nodded. "Doing another one?"

While they talked, Robert pulled Maggie aside.

"You better not leave the party until I know who's going with you. Either Jim or Paul. Just don't walk off into the dark." Robert scowled. "Buying that picture must have set the killer off. Bill's driving all the way over to the Department of Natural Resources to check on that boat. Says he can get a warrant as soon as he knows, or at the very least, interrogate the owner."

"He doesn't have a solid suspect yet?" Maggie asked.

"He will before the night is over. We'll all be tucked in our beds while he arrests the SOB. Hope whoever it is has gotten word that we're on to him and he's left the county."

"Well, last I heard, Bill figured a snowbird, just passing through, killed Cotton," Maggie pointed out.

"Not a chance. Cotton knew the person and maybe even worked with him," Robert declared.

Before he could elaborate, Marianna interrupted. "I talked to Hannah today. She's got some great ideas for the house. I'll see you next Tuesday." She took Robert's arm. "Come on, the band is playing great music." They walked away to the sound of an old Beach Boys tune.

Paul handed Maggie a glass of red wine. "What kind?" she asked.

Paul put his index finger to his lips. "I'm not telling," he said. "Let's see how well you know your wines."

Maggie sipped, then shrugged. "It's good, though," she said.

Paul swirled his glass in an imitation of Sherman. "It's crisp, dry, with just a hint of fruitiness."

Maggie smiled weakly at his joke, and she could tell he was disappointed in her response. She tried to work up a chuckle, but she couldn't get it past her throat.

She almost dropped her glass when Dickie Diamond grabbed her from behind and gave her a bear hug. "Just like old times," he said grimly. "The word at this party is to watch you. Heard you got a swat on the head this morning. You all right?"

"I'm fine, Dickie. The killer may be here tonight, but he's going to be picked up in the morning after Bill runs that boat's registration. Anyway, with everyone watching, he'd never get to me. And I'm convinced that if he wanted to kill me, he would have done it this morning. He could have smashed my skull like a raw egg."

Dickie grimaced at the imagery. "If Sallie Jo wadn't so pregnant, I'd stay with you night and day."

Maggie looked around. "Where is Sallie Jo? I haven't seen her."

"She got tired from all that party shower planning with Hannah today. Decided to stay home and put her feet up." Dickie exhaled noisily. "The mess with the Mary Grace has got me all hot and bothered. I gotta go to the mainland tonight, and it's hard now. But Robert said he'd let me use the Seaward Lady for a couple hours." He glanced at his watch. "I gotta go. I'll let the boys know I'm leavin'. All the waiters from the Red Eye are here. They don't need me." He walked away a few steps, and then walked back. "Look in on Sallie Jo tomorrow if you get time. She's kinda down 'cause she's goin' into town Friday, and she cain't come back till Junior gets here."

"You know for sure it's a boy?"

"Naw," Dickie answered. "Just ain't had any girls first in the family in three generations."

"There's always a first time," Maggie said with a laugh.

Maggie walked him to the boat, with Paul still trailing her, and she stood watching from the edge of an oyster bed as he maneuvered the Seaward Lady into open water.

She heard footsteps behind her, and whirled, then sighed with relief. It was only Jim.

"Let me know when you're ready to leave. I'll slip away and walk you home," he said.

"That won't be necessary," Paul answered quickly.

Maggie yawned. "I'm about ready for bed. Guess half the party will move to my house, what with everybody trying to watch over me." Her stomach rumbled, reminding her that she hadn't eaten since breakfast. "Let's shuck some oysters, guys. Your sauces look delicious, Jim."

At least thirty people had crowded around the shucking tables. Robert was explaining to an elderly snowbird about harvesting "only in the R months."

"A baby oyster is called a spat after the conception," he told the silver-haired lady. "Little ol' thing swims around for about two weeks, then settles in an old oyster shell." He paused to slip a fat, juicy oyster into his mouth, which he chased with a sip of pale ale. "You must throw the shells back in the water so the spats have a place to live until they're harvested."

Maggie had to smile. Robert certainly enjoyed having an audience, and the crowd around him was growing.

"Please go on," a chubby, middle-aged woman urged, looking up at Robert with admiration. "I've never thought about how these things happen. The only thing I know about oysters is they taste great."

Robert threw out his chest and continued his lecture. "These little gems eat single cell plants floating in the current. The amount of food and the kind they get determines the oyster's flavor and its color. These we got here tonight are special. Came from the best beds in the county." He waved his index finger back and forth under one giggling woman's nose. "Now, don't even bother to ask. I'm not giving my secret oyster spot away."

The crowd around him tittered, and Maggie feared the buttons on his shirt might pop if he puffed out his chest any farther.

Little Lavender was working hard to keep up with demand. The oysters were snatched up as soon as he pulled them, steaming, from the grill. Maggie didn't want to have to fight her way through the crowd to get her share. She would just wait until it thinned out some. She wandered a little way off, wanting peace and quiet. She sat on the pier and watched the tide. Her head was starting to ache again, and she hoped the cool breeze coming off the ocean might make her feel better.

Paul disappeared momentarily, but before long, he walked up and settled down beside her. "I have some news," he said. "Hannah heard from Bill. He's on his way back. Won't be here in time for the party. I'll walk you home whenever you're ready to go."

Maggie looked up and found herself surrounded. Apparently, nobody was letting her get far from sight tonight.

"I could walk you home," Jim volunteered, a hopeful look in his eye. Maggie heard other voices chime in. Granny's was a little louder than the rest.

Maggie's headache was getting worse, and she didn't have an appetite for oysters anymore. If she had felt better, she would have made a quip about leading Seaward's first October parade.

Paul helped her up and held onto her arm possessively. Jim and Hannah fell in behind; Granny followed, and Little Pig wobbled after her. Even Little Lav joined the procession. He reluctantly gave up the grill long enough to see Maggie safely home.

Some strangers at the party, misunderstanding the commotion, trailed after the lively group.

Lav grabbed Granny around the waist as they walked, and danced her down the path. Granny slapped at his hands impatiently, but before long, she was dancing along with him as enthusiastically as her rheumatism would allow. Soon, everyone except Maggie and Paul were dancing and hopping and laughing.

189

When Maggie and her entourage reached the yard, Possum ran to them, but she didn't go to Maggie. She was more interested in Little Pig. She circled the piglet, sniffing. Little Pig squealed a frantic protest and ran to Granny for help.

A man from Beaufort whom Maggie had never seen before asked if Seaward always had such fun parties. He had no idea that these people considered themselves Maggie's bodyguards.

Maggie just wanted to lie down. She tried to think of a gracious way to shoo them all away. "Good night, and thank you all for bringing me home," she shouted over the chattering and laughing. Hannah opened the door for her, and Maggie went straight to her sleeping porch. She fell onto the soft feather bed Hannah had covered with a cotton sheet.

"We'll talk in the morning," Maggie mumbled.

Hannah covered Maggie with a quilt and tucked it around her. "Bill will have the killer in custody by morning, and we'll be set to start our business. The worst is over now." She switched the light off and tiptoed away.

Tree frogs sang a lullaby, and Maggie drifted into a sound sleep.

Seventeen

Maggie turned over and pulled the covers tighter. When she had the sleeping porch built, she hadn't counted on the noise deer would make trying to get into the back yard to eat the Indian hawthorn. Possum heaved a big sigh and snorted in her sleep.

Maggie didn't have a clock on the porch, so she had no idea how long she had slept. She wondered if Bill was back on Seaward, and if he had made an arrest.

She hoped to go back to sleep quickly, but her mind seized on the Ribaut Inn project. Where would they find the perfect side tables? Maybe they would use the arrogantly shabby Pawleys Island summer houses as inspiration. Maggie liked that look.

The image of stargazer lilies and the jon boat leapt into her mind, and she was suddenly frightened. She sat up and listened for a moment. She heard nothing but the sounds of nocturnal wildlife and palmetto fronds rustling in the breeze.

Maggie chided herself for being jumpy. There was no reason left for the killer to come after her. Surely he knew that arrest was inevitable now that Bill had the boat's identification numbers. Anyway, Juan and Hannah were sleeping inside the house, just a shout away.

Still, she stared nervously through the screen into the dark. She considered going inside, but she dismissed the notion. It would have been nice, though, to have a big, strong man with her just now. But which man? She liked them both, and she wouldn't give up either until she was sure which one she wanted.

A portable phone next to her bed shrilled, and she almost cried out in fear before she realized where the sound was coming from. Who would call her in the dead of night? Maybe it was Bill calling to say he had nabbed the killer and she could rest easy.

She brought the receiver shakily to her ear.

"Jim here." She was momentarily annoyed at the late-night intrusion, but then relief washed over her. She felt less alone with Jim on the other end of the line. Hadn't she just been wishing for a protective man to make her feel safe?

"Sorry to bother you,'" he said, "but we've got a problem over here. Sallie Jo has gone into labor, and she's not due for another couple weeks. Can you bring your boat over to the marina? We have to get her to the mainland, and Dickie's not back yet. Will you come?"

Maggie didn't hesitate. "On my way." She had been so tired, she hadn't bothered to undress before tumbling into the daybed. She wouldn't even have to take time to throw on some clothes. She slipped on her shoes and grabbed her flashlight by the waterfront door as she ran out. *Poor Sallie must be so frightened,* she thought. *I'm glad I can help.*

She slipped on a nylon parka she kept on the boat and started the engine. Hannah's light came on, but there was no time to explain. "Damn, I wish I had a cell phone," Maggie mumbled. Then she realized that she could use Jim's to call Hannah later and let her know what was going on. Still, she felt a twinge of guilt because she knew Hannah would be worried.

Maggie adjusted the gears, and the Cash Floe sliced through water so calm, it looked like black velvet.

It took only a few minutes to get to Palmetto Bluff Marina. Maggie slid the Cash Floe into the spot where she and Hannah had found Cotton's body. So much had happened since then. Maggie heard someone running toward her from the darkness beyond the pier. Then a man came into view and pounded onto the dock. "Jim?" she called.

"It's me," he answered, and she breathed a sigh of relief. "Shut off your engine. It'll take a while to get Sallie Jo aboard."

Jim took Maggie's hand and helped her off the boat.

"Where is she?" Maggie asked. "Can the two of us get her into the boat, do you think? Has anyone called Beaufort Memorial? We can tie up at their dock."

Jim led her toward the parking lot, and Maggie looked around, trying to catch sight of Sallie Jo. She didn't hear any moans of pain. That had to be a good sign. Maybe her labor wasn't too far along yet.

Maggie whacked herself on the forehead with her palm. "We should have called Granny. She used to be a midwife. If Sallie's too far gone, we can take her over there. Granny's got an electric stove now, so we won't have to build a fire to boil water."

Jim stopped walking and looked down at her. "Stupid," he growled. "We won't be boiling any water."

Before Maggie could grasp what was happening, he grabbed her roughly by the arm and jerked her toward the marina building.

She went cold, and her legs shook so violently, she almost collapsed. But Jim pulled her against him and kept her moving. He dragged her across the parking lot and into the dark building. Maggie finally understood what was happening. She screamed and planted her feet. He slapped her hard across the face and flung her to the floor. "Shut up," he said with a deadly calm that chilled Maggie to the bone. He snatched the curtains closed and flipped on a light switch. Maggie caught sight of something glinting in his right hand—a stainless steel knife, the kind locals used to gut and fillet fish. She looked from the knife to his face. His eyes were wild and full of rage.

"Oh, no, Jim, not you," she moaned. "It couldn't have been you." At that moment, she felt more grief than fear.

His only response was another slap across her face. She scooted backwards, trying to put some distance between them.

"You're going to kill me," she whispered. It wasn't a question.

193

Jim pulled Maggie to her feet. He pulled back his right hand and slapped her hard. She collapsed and banged her head against the tile floor. She tasted something coppery and realized her mouth was bleeding.

Jim knelt beside Maggie, and the knife flashed in his hand.

"You look a lot like my first wife," he said, almost tenderly, "the woman I pushed into the Beaufort River."

"Why would you do that?" Maggie gasped.

"Meg kept nagging at me. She wanted more money for that restaurant in Savannah. Now it's mine. I always thought if I could get my own restaurant, I could become famous, maybe get my own TV show." He glared at her as if daring her to contradict him. "You have the same long, beautiful hair." Jim grabbed Maggie's hair and yanked. He ignored her cry of pain.

Maggie looked frantically around the room, but she could see no means of escape. Jim knelt between her and the door. Maybe she could reason with him.

"Talk to me, Jim," she pleaded. "Why did you kill Cotton? What did he ever do to you?"

He clenched his fists, and he began to rock back and forth on his knees.

"I can tell you're in pain inside," Maggie whispered. "Tell me what happened to you."

Maggie saw that he was about to swing again, and she twisted her body to avoid the blow. But his fist caught her squarely on the left shoulder. Her arm went numb, and tears sprang to her eyes.

If she could just stay alive until someone came to open the marina, Maggie thought desperately, she might be saved. Surely it was almost dawn, and the marina opened very early. She scooted just a fraction farther from him and tried again to get him talking. "The sauces at the roast were a great success," she said. "But, look, you've spilled more mustard sauce on your smock. Guess you really needed that bleach."

"Stupid," he barked. "You know stains from stargazer lilies won't come out." He rubbed his palm hard against the yellow stains on his chest, as if he were trying to rub them away. "I had to honor Cotton. That's what the lilies were for." He looked Maggie dead in the eye. "I'll honor you, too."

He held the point of the knife against her right arm. Maggie could see his hand was shaking. Then the blade pierced her windbreaker and sliced down the length of her arm. It seemed to Maggie that it was slicing her flesh in slow motion, that it took forever for Jim to pull it back. She couldn't seem to move. She watched blood stream down her hand and puddle on the floor. She wondered why she didn't feel anything, and then the pain hit, and she screamed. She tried to crawl away, on hands and knees, but Jim grabbed her bleeding arm and pulled her back.

"Cotton found out," Jim said calmly. "Almost ruined all my plans."

Maggie tried desperately to focus on what he was saying. "Found out what, Jim?" The puddle on the floor was widening, and her whole body trembled. But she forced herself to speak softly. "You can tell me. Trust me with your secret."

"Owning my own restaurant in Savannah. Cotton helped me build the antique mahogany bar. Beautiful work." He looked at Maggie mournfully. "Too bad you won't ever get to see it. You would have really liked it. See, Cotton wanted a paycheck every week. Thought I didn't have money, but I took all I wanted from those people in Georgetown. Cotton said that was embezzlement." Jim waved the knife in the air, and Maggie followed it with her eyes. "Those people owned a chicken franchise. They didn't need that money. I just helped myself to the till, a little at a time, until I got enough for a down payment on my own place."

Maggie tried to ease herself backwards, but Jim caught the movement out of the corner of his eyes. "Stay where you are, or I'll cut you up and feed you to the fish."

Maggie forced herself to sit still while he rocked and babbled. "Cotton planned to tell the police what I had done. I couldn't let him do that. Told him to meet me here after I finished for the night. He wanted me to confess and pay the money back. I would have paid him to keep quiet, but the fool wouldn't take the money. I can't go to jail. When I kill Stella, Penny will need me to take care of her."

"So Stella is your daughter's mother?"

"Stella, my second wife, was supposed to run the restaurant for me, but now she says she'll turn me in if I don't sign it over to her."

He looked at Maggie, and his eyes blazed.

"Everything should have gone right," he said. "I was almost home free. But people keep getting in my way!"

His voice was getting louder, and his rocking became more frantic.

"So you got Cotton in the boat somehow, and you killed him." Jim flashed Maggie a menacing look. "Well, what choice did you have?" she added quickly.

"Chandler had paid Cotton all that money for the work he did at the church, but I didn't know that until after Cotton was already dead. Seemed a shame to let it go to waste, so I took it for the restaurant."

Maggie nodded. "Of course," she said. She felt weak and dizzy, but she couldn't pass out now.

"I liked Cotton," Jim said sadly. "He was a good guy. I didn't want to just dump his body somewhere, so I hid him in the freezer. But I couldn't keep him there long. So I dumped him somewhere I knew he would be found, and I hid the boat. But that bitch Stella

196

found it, and she painted it, for godsake! I had to cover up the numbers. That's why I took the painting."

Jim stopped rocking and rubbed at the stain on his smock again. "It won't come out," he said to Maggie, and his words sounded almost like a sob.

"Take the smock off," she said, trying to sound sympathetic. "Just take it off."

Jim pulled it over his head and Maggie saw a black Palmetto Bluff Marina T-shirt underneath. The word "Bluff" was misspelled.

Maggie felt faint, but she knew if she lost consciousness now, she would die. She tried to pay attention while Jim ranted on.

"Cotton wasn't very smart," Jim said. "He kept his life savings stashed at his house. Didn't trust banks. He told me he was gonna give some of it to you for safekeeping. So right after he died, I went to his trailer and found a box full of money. I needed that money. But then I thought that if you had all that cash, the police would think you had killed Cotton and robbed him." Jim pointed the knife at Maggie like an accusing finger. "But you didn't tell anybody about the money. You hid it. You wanted to keep it for yourself. If you tell me where it is, maybe I won't have to hurt your friend Hannah."

"You're the one who trashed Althea's house. Were you looking for more money?"

Jim stood up abruptly. "I'm done talking," he said. "It's almost daylight, and we don't have much time. I'm not going to make the same mistake with you that I made with Cotton. Nobody will find your body."

"Jim, you're not thinking straight," Maggie pleaded. "Bill already knows about the boat, and he has the identification numbers. Killing me won't save you."

Jim seemed not to hear. "We'll take the Cash Floe out to St. Helena Sound. You're bleeding like chum. The sharks will come from miles around."

He jerked Maggie from the floor, and the room spun around her. He threw her over his shoulder, carried her to the boat, and dragged her aboard.

Maggie slumped to the deck. She heard the engine start, and she drifted into unconsciousness.

Eighteen

Maggie opened her eyes, then shut them immediately against the bright sunshine. She shaded her face and tried again. Jim was at the helm.

They didn't appear to be in open water yet, but Maggie knew they were headed toward the Atlantic.

She moved slowly onto her hands and knees and groaned in pain. Her head hurt so badly, it was hard to think. She was bruised and sore, but at least the cut on her arm had almost stopped bleeding. She crawled to a seat and pulled herself up.

Jim turned to watch as she collapsed onto the cushion. His face was streaked with her blood.

"Sorry I can't offer you coffee. You look like you could use some. Well, I guess it's time to get you tied up," he said casually. "You're too good a swimmer for me to just toss you over. Even with all that blood on you, somebody might find you before the sharks do. Can't have that." He looked around the boat. "Let's see, where do you keep the rope? I hope you won't struggle, Maggie." He gave her a reproachful look. "I've already got blood on my clothes, and I have to be back at the Tabby by eleven for the lunch crowd."

Maggie heard the radio squawk, and she wondered if she could get to it and yell for help before Jim could stop her.

"Don't even think it," he snapped, waving the knife.

Maggie looked around, trying to formulate a plan. Could she jump overboard and swim to safety? It didn't seem likely. If this was a shark-infested area, they would smell her blood, and she would be done for. And even if the sharks didn't get her, Maggie was weak and groggy, and she knew she wouldn't last long in the chilly water.

"All right, Maggie, let's don't prolong this. Where is the rope?"

Maggie knew that pleading with him was a waste of breath, and there was no way that anyone could come to her rescue, since no one knew where she was. But neither was she just going to give up and let him toss her overboard without a fight.

"The rope is stowed under this seat," she said weakly.

"What did you say? Speak up!" Jim ordered.

Maggie took a long breath and repeated, louder this time, "The rope is stowed under this seat."

Jim smiled at her lovingly, just as he had smiled so many times before. But anyone looking into his eyes at that moment would know he was insane. "Well, get it out for me," he said as calmly as if he had asked her to get him a drink of water. "And don't try anything. I'd have to carve you up some more before I throw you overboard. Let's make this as quick and clean as we can."

She stood slowly, tossed the cushion away, and lifted the seat. She frantically surveyed the contents, hoping to find a weapon of some kind. There was no gun onboard, she knew, but maybe there was something.

Jim watched impatiently and then left the wheel and walked toward her.

"Stalling won't do you any good," he said.

He was just a few yards away when she saw the flare gun Robert had given her. She fumbled with the flares and finally managed to get the device loaded. She glanced over her shoulder and saw that Jim was getting closer. She tried to remember Robert's instructions, but her mind wouldn't focus on anything except the madman advancing on her. And then she remembered what Robert had said about the safety mechanism. She pulled a lever and heard a snap. If she had done it right, the gun was ready to fire.

She whirled and pointed the flare gun at Jim's chest.

He backed up a few steps, looking mildly surprised, and he threw back his head and laughed. Maggie saw dried blood in his hair and on his hands, and his pants were blotched with red.

Her hands shook so hard, she wasn't sure she could hit him, even at this range. And even if she did, would it stop him or just make him mad?

"I don't want to hurt you, Jim. Just don't come any closer." Her throat was so dry, she could only croak the warning.

His eyes narrowed, and he took a step forward.

Maggie gripped the flare gun tighter. "I mean it, Jim," she said softly, and tears filled her eyes. "Please don't make me do this."

He lunged. Maggie closed her eyes, turned her face away, and pulled the trigger. She heard a swooshing sound, and something that sounded like fireworks crackling, and she heard Jim scream. She opened her eyes, dreading what she would see. Jim's T-shirt was smoldering, and some sort of thick gel dripped down his face and arms.

"It burns!" he yelled.

He tore off the T-shirt, and his skin was blackened and blistered underneath. He let out a bellow of pain and rage. His eyes locked with Maggie's briefly, and the agony she saw there made her sob.

He ran to the side of the boat and jumped over. She heard a splash.

She didn't look into the water. Her only thought was to get the boat going and get away before he could climb back on board. She stumbled to the wheel and hit the gearshift, causing the boat to lurch forward. It was only when the Cash Floe was moving rapidly away that she looked back for Jim. He was paddling frantically and screaming for help.

And then it occurred to her that he was covered in her blood.

She saw a dark fin break the water just behind him and another to his right.

She killed the engine and tried to think. She couldn't let him die like that, but if she went back for him and let him on the boat, he would kill her.

And then the sharks attacked. Jim screamed once—it was the most horrible sound Maggie had ever heard—and he went under.

Through tears, Maggie started the boat, checked her navigational system, and picked up the radio's microphone. She told the Coast Guard to have a doctor ready when she reached land, and she asked the dispatcher to send a search team for Jim, though she doubted they would find any trace of him.

"Shall we send a rescue team for you?" the dispatcher asked.

Maggie wiped her eyes and pressed the transmit button. "No, I can make it to Beaufort on my own," she said.

When she pulled into the Beaufort marina, Bill and a doctor were standing on the dock to meet her.

And so was Paul. When he caught sight of her, he opened his arms wide.

About the author

L inda Shirley Robertson lives on an island off the coast of South Carolina with her husband, Henry. She was born in Greenville, South Carolina, and received her B.A. degree from Winthrop University. Ms. Robertson's work has been published in regional and national publications. In 1982 she co-authored South Carolina's International Greenville. In recent years she has written a series of short stories depicting Southern life with wit and authenticity. *Murder Rocks the Boat* is her second Maggie Stewart novel, which follows the first in the series, *Murder Swings the Tide.*

Colophon

Tabby Manse

Coastal Villages Press is dedicated to helping
to preserve the timeless values of traditional
places along America's Atlantic coast—
building houses to endure through
the centuries; living in harmony
with the natural environment;
honoring history, culture,
family and friends—
and helping to
make
these
values
relevant
today.
This
book
was
completed on
December 15, 2004, at Beaufort, South Carolina.
It was designed and set by George Graham Trask in Adobe
Garamond, a rendition of a typeface created by
Claude Garamond in Paris in 1530.